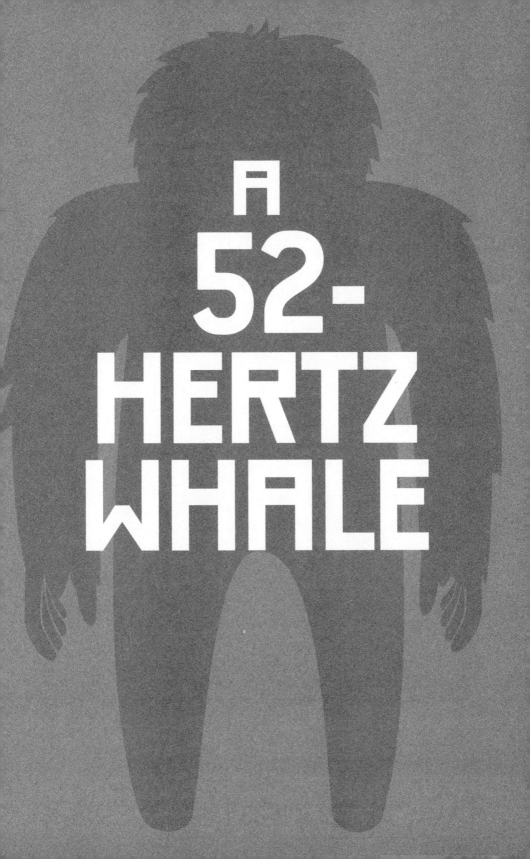

A
52-HERTZ
WHALE

BILL SOMMER AND
NATALIE HANEY TILGHMAN

carolrhoda LAB

MINNEAPOLIS

Quote on back of jacket: "52-hertz whale," *Wikipedia*, February 12, 2015,
https://en.wikipedia.org/wiki/52-hertz_whale (February 12, 2015).

Carolrhoda Lab™
An imprint of Carolrhoda Books
A division of Lerner Publishing Group, Inc.
241 First Avenue North
Minneapolis, MN 55401 USA

For reading levels and more information, look up this title
at www.lernerbooks.com.

The image in this book is used with the permission of: © iStockphoto.com/bldlss.

Main body text set in Janson Text LT Std 10/15.
Typeface provided by Linotype AG.

Library of Congress Cataloging-in-Publication Data

Tilghman, Natalie Haney.
    A 52-hertz whale / Natalie Haney Tilghman and Bill Sommer.
      pages cm
    Summary: Reveals, through emails from various people, the growing
  connection between sixteen-year-old James, who is obsessed with the fate of
  a juvenile humpback whale he adopted, and Darren, a would-be filmmaker
  who once did community service in James's Special Education classroom.
    ISBN 978-1-4677-7917-3 (lb : alk. paper) — ISBN 978-1-4677-8811-3
  (eb pdf)
    [1. Interpersonal relations—Fiction. 2. Humpback whale—Fiction.
  3. Whales—Fiction. 4. People with mental disabilities—Fiction. 5. Email—
  Fiction.] I. Sommer, Bill. II. Title. III. Title: Fifty-two hertz whale.
  PZ7.1.T55Aag 2015
  [Fic]—dc23   2015001618

Manufactured in the United States of America
1 – BP – 7/15/15

For my boys, especially RHT IV,
and for Mom
—NHT

For Mom and Dad
—Bill Jr.

SEPTEMBER 2012

From: whaleboy4ever@gmail.com
To: the.darren.olmstead@gmail.com
Date: September 6, 2012 at 11:27 PM
Subject: Help

Hi Darren:

You probably don't remember me.

We met like a year ago in the Resource Room at Glenside Middle School. You helped us film a completely ridiculous advertisement for a new soft drink. This was some sort of "exercise" to help our Social Skills group learn to work together, I guess. The result: Gabber Aid, "the beverage that speaks volumes." I have to say that the only thing more embarrassing than being in the Social Skills group is to have it documented on film. Still, your camera work was impeccable.

By any chance, do you remember Sam Pick from the Resource Room? The kid who would wear a different shirt with a high-resolution picture of a spider on it each day of the week? Sam doesn't have to go to the Resource Room anymore now that we're at Carlsburg High. Last year, Sam and I would watch Jacques Cousteau DVDs after school. I taught him stuff like a humpback whale's heart can weigh three times as much as a human being's or that flukes are like fingerprints—no two are the same. These days, though, Sam is busy playing backup goalie on the soccer team with people like Charlie Coxson. This Coxson character is a junior, the soccer captain, and his PSAT scores are so good that he's in Mensa. So it's easy to see why Sam thinks he's cool. That leaves me alone, listening to humpback songs on CD after school or tracking my adopted whale, Salt, on the Greater New England Whale Conservatory's website as he makes his annual migration to Argentina.

Which is why I'm emailing you. On your last day with our Social Skills group, you said if I ever needed help, I could contact you via this email. Well, I need help.

About a week ago, Salt's tracking dot was stalled in the Gulf of Maine. I was pretty certain that Salt was lost or separated from his pod. So I tried calling the scientists at the Greater New England Whale Conservatory (GNEWC) to alert them, but whoever answered—maybe it was the janitor—blamed the inactivity on a technical glitch. He also mentioned that juveniles don't migrate every year. (As if I didn't know that? I mean, really.)

Anyway, it was clear to me that this guy at the Greater New England Whale Conservatory didn't know a marine mammal emergency when he saw one. We're talking about a member of an endangered species here—all alone and lost in 41,500,000 square miles of ocean. Anyway, when Salt's tracking dot started moving again a couple of days later, it was headed in the wrong direction—toward New England's rocky coast instead of south toward the Carolinas. At this point, I think that Salt's echolocation is seriously impaired, which might cause him to beach.

What should I do?

Sincerely,

James Turner

P.S. How are you? What are you doing these days?

From: the.darren.olmstead@gmail.com
To: whaleboy4ever@gmail.com
Date: September 7, 2012 at 11:58 PM
Subject: RE: Help

James!

Good to hear from you, dog. Bummer about your giant mammalian buddy. Unfortunately, I'm no whale expert and don't know what to tell you about getting your boy turned in the right direction. Heck, I might be even more lost than him these days. Might have to go to the doc and get my echolocation checked out.

Sorry. I hope things are good otherwise.

Take it breezy,

Darren

P.S. Thanks for noticing my camera work.

From: whaleboy4ever@gmail.com
To: the.darren.olmstead@gmail.com
Date: September 8, 2012 at 7:27 AM
Subject: RE: Help

Dear Darren,

I have to apologize if you just gave me your email just to be polite. Kind of like when people ask, "How are you?" but don't want to know the answer. One time, when I was little, this grocery clerk asked me how I was doing, and I said that I peed my pants at school and the nurse had to give me a pair of jeans that were two sizes too big and I was thinking of running away, maybe jumping a plane from Philly to Patagonia to watch the annual whale migration. "But he's fine," my mom said. The clerk smiled and I realized that Mom had given the right answer.

Anyway, I wrote you because I thought I remembered you mentioning something about an article that you read online featuring a historically significant blue whale poop—the largest on record—and how it was pretty cool that floating feces can end up fertilizing the entire ocean, keeping the ecosystem in good working order. You seemed to get the fact that humans need whales. And I figured you'd understand how Salt's untimely disappearance directly affects us all.

Sincerely,

James Turner

From: the.darren.olmstead@gmail.com
To: lwoodward1million@gmail.com
Date: September 9, 2012 at 1:15 AM
Subject: FWD: Help

Check it, dog. Here's the email I was telling you about. It's from this kid at the school where I paid my debt to society last year. Poor li'l dude must be lonely as hell!

From: ktolmsteadmommy@gmail.com
To: the.darren.olmstead@gmail.com
Date: September 9, 2012 at 11:42 AM
Subject: Checking in

Hey D,

Just checking in to see how you're holding up. Talked to Mom the other day, and from what it sounded like, the worst of it's behind you. Just remember that time is your friend here.

Nothing much to report. John's company didn't give him any paternity leave, so once Mom left, I was on my own for a few weeks and I was starting to go slightly insane, I think, so he just took a week off and stayed around the house and helped out. It was SO nice to have an adult conversation before 6 p.m. every day. Bad news is, Good-bye vacation. Probably won't get to see you at Christmas unless you want to come out here. Winters in Milwaukee get a much worse rap than they deserve. (Ha! No they don't. They get exactly the rap they deserve. Can't lie to my li'l bro.)

Gracie's down for her nap and Robby's just lying here staring up at me as I type this. I've got some awfully cute photos of my two little munchkins that I'll send you for a little added cheering up. Mom told me you're off Facebook for the time being—smart move, I wouldn't be able to resist looking at her pictures either—so I'll put a bunch of pics of the twins in an email when I get a chance.

Love you,
Katie

From: lwoodward1million@gmail.com
To: the.darren.olmstead@gmail.com
Date: September 9, 2012 at 4:15 PM
Subject: RE: FW: Help

Lonelier than the dude who emailed the dude he sleeps down the hall from at one in the morning? Hey-o! What a burn. Take Darren to the Burn Unit!

Also, another reminder: doing your dishes is not a once-a-week chore. It's an every-time-you-use-dishes chore. Comprendé?

Luke

From: the.darren.olmstead@gmail.com
To: whaleboy4ever@gmail.com
Date: September 10, 2012 at 2:45 PM
Subject: RE: Help

Hey there James,

I don't know if I was just being polite when I gave you my email address, as I have no recollection of doing so. Due to some recent revelations in self-knowledge, though, I'm guessing what really happened was that I felt some brief but powerful surge of emotion toward you and gave you my email address. In the intervening months, all of my emotional enthusiasm has gotten sucked into a black hole, to the point that I forgot the entire incident.

Anyway, as far as the giant whale poop, I think you've got me confused with someone else. I actually have to work hard to block out thoughts of marine feces every time I go in the ocean, otherwise I can't enjoy my swim. So I definitely wasn't doing a happy dance over a colossal whale turd.

But I do remember helping out in that Social Skills class and filming you in the Gabber Aid commercial. I remember you really nailing the part where you're standing there looking back and forth as two kids have a conversation and you're totally left out in the cold until you chug that Gabber Aid and make a brilliant conversational entrance like, "Hey guys, what's up?" Easier said than done, I know. Wait—actually, the saying is the doing in that case. Which is the hard part for folks in your situation, right? Anyway, not easily said. I have trouble empathizing on that particular difficulty, as I'm rarely at a loss for words. Honestly, my life would probably be a lot better off if I lost a few words every now and then.

And of course I remember Sam. I applaud him for broadening his horizons with soccer, though it's a bummer you guys aren't as close anymore. You know what they say (actually you probably don't, since you're fourteen, so I'm going to tell you): The only constant in life is change. He moved on. You might have to as well. Same thing happened to me a while back.

As for how I'm doing: When I met you, I was back in Philly on a little, um, hiatus from college, but after the year ended I headed back to Los Angeles and finally graduated with a Bachelor's in film and television production from USC. Unsure of what to do next, I threw together a ragtag crew of misfits and we said, "Screw the establishment, we're going to make a movie on our own terms." So we did, the critics loved it, and now we've been asked to take over the entire Marvel comics film franchise. We're considering it.

Spoiler alert: None of that happened.

Except for me getting my degree. Now I'm a PA (showbiz abbrev. of production assistant) on an absolutely wretched family sitcom here in the City of Angels, but I spend most of my time daydreaming topics for the great documentary I will someday make. Ironically, this gig makes the days of filming commercials for imaginary social-skill–enhancing drinks seem like the golden age of my filmmaking life. Contrary to popular belief, starting out in Hollywood isn't just about bringing coffee to important people. That's just the most interesting part.

So, about this whale. First, are you sure it was the janitor who answered the phone? That's not very common. If so, kudos to him for being what sounds to me like a pretty knowledgeable janitor, even if he proves incorrect about the fate of your whale friend. Unfortunately, I have no idea what your next step should be in this matter, other than calling and asking to speak to someone besides the suspiciously well-informed janitor. As far as the dot moving in the wrong direction, for now I'd have faith in Salt to find his right path. Sometimes the young have to wander lost for a while before eventually getting it all figured out (at least this is what I'm telling my mom right now to get her off my back about law school, but that's a different story). Also, don't pooh-pooh the idea of just kicking it solo for a while. Take it from Mr. Darren, the guy who has endured a maddening number of creepy moments with people he met from answering Craigslist roommate-needed ads. But in all seriousness, give it a few days, call back, and see what they say.

Best,

Darren

From: whaleboy4ever@gmail.com
To: the.darren.olmstead@gmail.com
Date: September 11, 2012 at 4:13 PM
Subject: RE: Help

Dear Darren,

I wanted to tell you that I called the Greater New England Whale Conservatory back like you suggested. The receptionist (who sounded suspiciously like the janitor I spoke with previously) put me through to the Development Department, then some woman asked me if I wanted to renew my adoption of Salt. Get this: the annual fee is $10 higher than the year before. I told the woman that I refused to open my wallet again until I got more information on Salt's current whereabouts and health from a marine researcher or scientist. Funny how then I got promptly transferred.

The scientist I spoke with confirmed my hunch that Salt is indeed separated from his pod. According to said scientist, there is some reason to be concerned. In the past two months, at least one other juvenile beached in the same area where Salt is currently swimming. The scientist said he is puzzled as to what is pulling the whales toward the dangerous shallows and the shore. I left the scientist my email and the scientist promised to update me. We shall see.

Sincerely yours,
James Turner

From: whaleboy4ever@gmail.com
To: the.darren.olmstead@gmail.com
Date: September 12, 2012 at 4:15 PM
Subject: Cease and Desist?

Dear Darren,

I hate to bother you again, especially because I think I may have misremembered your interest in whale poop. The thing is that, right now, I don't really have anyone else to bother. Still, bothering is bothering, so I will cease and desist if you just say the word.

Before I do so, you advised me to "move on" from my friendship with Sam. Since you seem to have experience in this arena, how exactly does one go about "moving on"?

Sincerely,

James Turner

From: sduckett@gnewc.org
To: pbrammer@gnewc.org
Date: September 12, 2012 at 4:38 PM
Subject: Stanley Duckett from GNEWC

Peter,

This is the first time in 10 years I'm using this email address they gave me. Took me 5 minutes just to type the subject. Sorry to bother you, especially with your father just passed and all. But Jan's been out with the flu and I'm covering the front desk in addition to all my normal stuff like fixing the AC in Howard's suite for the 50th time. Damn Indian summer. I guess the office wants to send you some flowers, trouble is I can't find your address in Jan's mess.

Could you send? Also a box came in the mail for you. Should I just put it on your desk? Gotta go lock up.

—Stanley P. Duckett

From: pbrammer@gnewc.org
To: sduckett@gnewc.org
Date: September 12, 2012 at 4:56 PM
Subject: RE: Stanley Duckett from GNEWC

Dear Stanley,

Thanks for the condolences. My address is 712 Overlook Lane, Woods Hole, MA 02543. I'm out on leave, and of course, one of our echo sounders is malfunctioning right when we need to track a wayward juvenile in distress in the same area where we've had previous issues with beaching the past few weeks. Thanks to our real-time tracking feature, I'm getting calls from concerned donors like this one teenage kid who acts like Salt is his best friend. That box might contain the part we've been waiting for. Can you open it and let me know?

Best wishes,

Peter

Peter Brammer, PhD

Marine Researcher

Greater New England Whale Conservancy

From: jolmstead@hensonacademyfl.org
To: tonyapholmes543@gmail.com, (56 others)
Date: September 12, 2012 at 5:35 PM
Subject: Introduction

Dear Parents,

Please pardon my lateness in sending this letter. I apologize for waiting until two games into the season to formally introduce myself to you all. My name is Jack Olmstead, and I'm the new head football coach here at Henson Academy, I'm proud to say.

1-1 wasn't the start I had in mind, but Grover Cleveland was a tough squad, and some of our growing pains as a team made themselves extra painful during that game. I accept full responsibility for the loss. With the nonconference games behind us, we are ready to embark into conference play. Notice I say "we." Because you guys are just as much a part of this team as me and the players are, even though you don't watch endless hours of game film and chart out X's and O's like me, and you don't put on pads and a helmet and put in a mouth guard and lace up your cleats like your kids. As parents, you guys are like my coaches off the field. Your actions and words shape the 35 young men (and 1 young lady) who step onto that field every Friday night for the next 10 weeks. (Notice that 10 more weeks of play assumes we reach the Florida Class A2 state championship game. Our goal is nothing less. We here at Henson Academy aim for greatness.)

I urge you to please do all you can to help your player be the best they can be this season. Now you're probably saying, "Whoa, Coach O, I don't know a bubble screen from a double read-option play." Don't worry. Me and Coach Erickson have that covered. Where you come in is helping your player be mentally and physically prepared to succeed in practices and games. Here are some suggestions.

Diet: For the next 10 weeks, burgers should be eaten from a plate, no bread. Mac 'n' cheese will be deleted from your player's vocabulary. Mac 'n' chicken breast with two servings of leafy green vegetables and carrots? Sure. Mac 'n' cheese, no. Soda? Might as well call McDowell High now and let them know they can start printing up their repeat championship T-shirts.

Sleep: Your players need sleep. There's tons of research on this, which I would oblige to send you if you want. So if it's possible, please consider turning off all Wi-Fi after 10:30 p.m. on weeknights and consider purchasing an entertainment cabinet that can be equipped with a lock (to be locked after 10:30 p.m. on weeknights) to remove the temptation of video games. I can send links to items on eBay that fit this description, or if that is not a monetarily possible option, you could simply confiscate the video game systems after 10:30 p.m. on weeknights and store them in your bedroom until the next day.

Discipline: Lastly, it's important to your player's success that he or she feel supported in this journey we call a season. When your player messes up, in a game or in life, you must make it clear that, as regrettable as that mistake is, the next play or the next day supplies your player with another chance at success. I am not proposing that disobedience such as curfew breaking, backtalk, or the eating of processed carbohydrates should go unremarked. I am instead imploring you to help your player understand that the punishment for their infractions serves what I call an upfield-downfield purpose. The punishment is in response (upfield) to the infraction, but it also serves to help your player succeed when his or her next opportunity presents itself (downfield). Otherwise it would be pointless.

Please contact me if you have any further questions. As it is my first year as coach here at Henson, I look forward to getting to know each and every one of you and seeing you in the stands each week now that conference play has begun.

Thank you very much,

Jack Olmstead

Head Football Coach, Henson Academy

From: the.darren.olmstead@gmail.com
To: whaleboy4ever@gmail.com
Date: September 12, 2012 at 5:48 PM
RE: Cease and Desist?

Hola J-World,

Patience, young caterpillar. I ain't trying to blow you off. I just didn't know what to say about the whale. Still don't. But I'm glad you're fighting the powers that be by withholding that donation. I hope it gets their attention.

Look, I probably should never have said anything in the first place, but since you apparently actually seem to listen to what I say—a rarity for me these days given my employment and ex-girlfriend situations—let me clarify my suggestion regarding your friend Sam.

You guys used to be buddies, and you felt a connection with him because you guys were really into creatures; you knew absurd amounts of information about whales and he was obsessed with spiders. Your friendship surely included other elements, but the creature facts were something you guys fed off of, something that made you feel understood by the other. That's why people have friends: to feel understood by people they feel they can understand. That's why the teacher Mrs. Whatshername from that Social Skills group had you guys spend so much time paying attention to people's facial expressions, tone of voice, choice of words, posture and other body language, et cetera. It will help you understand them better and allow you to feel like you're part of the tribe. Or better yet, the pod. Which can be a nice thing, especially if you're on some big journey trying to swim a gazillion miles down to South America or whatever. That make sense?

So let's try to understand this Charlie Coxson character. Real good soccer player, apparently. And for some reason, be it a shared interest in soccer or something else, Sam feels a connection with him. That's something you can't control. You can't go around trying to break them up. Trust me. I know. Firsthand.

But I actually wasn't advising you to move on from your friendship with Sam, just to understand that it's an option. There are others. One would be to see if you can forge a connection with Charlie too, because by understanding Charlie, you might understand why Sam likes him, and thus understand Sam better, which, to review, makes you a better friend. (Bein' a friend ain't easy, eh?!)

Or you might not like Charlie. Then you have to decide whether it's worth putting up with Charlie in order to be around Sam. Either way, you also might consider trying to be a little more like Charlie. IMPORTANT: I'm not saying dress like him or burn your whale books and start watching YouTube clips of Messi and Ronaldo all day, but it might be worth emulating what attracts Sam to him, as long as you emulate good things and not bad ones. E.g., if Sam thinks it's cool that Charlie is a real pro at kitten-punching, don't go and do that. But giving soccer a chance or laughing when Charlie tells a good joke might not be a bad move. Is any of this making sense?

In summary: being open to Sam=good. Punching kittens=bad.

As for my own experience with moving on from a relationship, I don't want to get into it because, unfortunately, all this stuff gets even more complicated as you get older and participate in dramatically different kinds of sleepovers.

Best,

Darren

P.S. I'm sorry to hear about your whale buddy's predicament, but I must reiterate that, while I may know a little about teenage drama from my own wretched experience of it, I don't know nothin 'bout no teenage whales. Sorry I can't help there. Good luck.

From: sduckett@gnewc.org
To: pbrammer@gnewc.org
Date: September 13, 2012 at 1:30 PM
RE: Stanley Duckett from GNEWC

Peter,

Well, I opened the box. It's mostly bubble wrap. No sonar. Just a seashell with a note that says "Oliva reticularis. Netted Olive. Caribbean Islands." Plays a sea song when you hold it up to your ear. Two more boxes came today. What should I do with them?

—Stanley P. Duckett

P.S. Actually kind of like this email thing. You can't hear my stutter or see that I'm 5'4" and probably need to lose around 60 lbs.

P.P.S. The real-time tracking feature for the donors is broken, I think, and IT Ron is in the Galápagos Islands on vacation.

From: pbrammer@gnewc.org
To: sduckett@gnewc.org
Date: September 13, 2012 at 2:53 PM
RE: Stanley Duckett from GNEWC

Hi Stanley,

Thanks to everyone in the office for the cheerful bouquet. The lilies have my house smelling like my ex-wife. Sorry, I haven't returned many of the calls you forwarded to my cell. Too busy cleaning out my parents' apartment and fighting the urge to keep everything (Dad's bowling shoes that smell like his Gold Bond foot powder and Mom's botany books with pages dog-eared). Today, I found some old pictures of me and my kid sister, Elsie, taken in Oregon on vacation when we were just kids. In one, there's a clam on Elsie's palm and she's grinning like the shell is made from 14-karat gold. I can't remember the last time I saw Elsie smile like that. Come to think of it, I can't remember the last time I saw Elsie— period. Maybe two years ago after her third stint in rehab. I think we met at Friendly's or something and she ordered her favorite sundae—butterscotch (which she called "hopscotch" when we were kids). The person eating that sundae was the Old Elsie. My Elsie. Otherwise, I didn't know what to make of the woman in front of me, reeking of cigarette smoke and hairspray, talking about twelve steps, her latest tattoo, and plans to finish her college degree, and pulling at her shirt sleeves so I couldn't see the scars on her wrists. I don't know why I am telling you all this except that I don't know how to get in touch with her because her last known number is disconnected. And Elsie doesn't even know about Dad.

If you could, please open the two boxes. I am really hoping that it is that piece of sonar equipment. The situation isn't looking good for our whale friend, and it keeps me up at night (along with the incessant chiming of the grandfather clock in my parents' apartment that insists on ringing every single hour despite my best attempts to disable it).

Best,

Peter

P.S. Was there any return address on that seashell box? And are we sure it was meant for me? I wasn't expecting anything and, frankly, I'm kind of puzzled.

From: whaleboy4ever@gmail.com
To: the.darren.olmstead@gmail.com
Date: September 13, 2012 at 9:57 PM
RE: Cease and Desist?

Dear Darren:

Thanks for the advice about Sam.

Yesterday, I got this phone message. It sounded like Sam, but voices in the background made it hard to hear. He said something like: "Hey buddy, what's up? Just wanted to see . . . hang out tomorrow after school. Meet me . . . seventh period at my locker. I've got . . . show you. Later, man."

I listened to the message a couple times to make sure I heard right. Because the last time Sam called me was the end of eighth grade when he wanted help feeding his tarantula, Sparky, who ended up passing away over the summer. On the fifth listen, I realized Sam wanted to hang out with me again. And I started daydreaming, thinking how we might head to Sam's house after school and search his backyard for spiders, just like old times, peeling back layers of tree bark until one of us discovered a wolf spider. Then I imagined us up in Sam's room looking up the scientific names of the specimens we caught. I even started to convince myself that

Sam would want to quit the soccer team.

Spoiler alert: None of that happened.

Today, I went to Sam's locker after seventh period like the message said. But Sam wasn't alone. He was with the entire soccer team. Long story short, the whole thing was a hoax. Coxson made Sam destroy my whale diorama, an extra credit project for Biology class. There was pornographic graffiti on some of my lobtailing shots and the habitat itself was pretty smashed up. My one and only picture of Salt was gone. Someone slapped Sam on the back and welcomed him to the team. That someone was Craig Smith, who up until last year was a habitual nose-picker. Now, he's a starting forward. Anyway, I guess this whole diorama disaster was a kind of initiation process. Team building. More like brainwashing if you ask me.

Sincerely,

James Turner

P.S. Salt's location remains 170 miles east of Cape Cod. Not good. Not good at all.

From: ciaosoph@gmail.com
To: saraannblakely@gmail.com
Date: September 13, 2012 at 10:03 PM
Subject: James Turner

Dear Sara:

Oh my god. It was the saddest thing today.

Don't tell anyone (even Becky) but you know my neighbor James Turner, right? From Bio and Italian???? My nonna tutors him in Italian and she says he's the only person she knows who can make biscotti as good as hers.

Anyway, after seventh period today, I'm at my locker and

James is unpacking his backpack and Sam Pick comes over with some of the soccer guys like Coxson and Craig Smith. The name on Sam's soccer jersey reads "Li'l Prick" instead of "Li'l Pick". Someone added the makeshift r with black tape.

Coxson shoves Sam forward and goes, "Tell him what's up, Prick."

And Sam says, "I got something for you, James."

James is studying the floor and his mouth is moving like he's counting the tiles. Coxson claps his hands near James's face, trying to get his attention.

Once James looks up, Sam presents him with his totally destroyed diorama from Bio. Hearts are drawn around photos of whales with red lipstick. And this is gross, but some of the whales have privates drawn in. Coxson is laughing like the annoying hyena he is. (BTW, does that kid even have a first name? What is it?)

And then, James belts out this sad song that sounds as if it was composed by the last whale on earth. I felt so bad for him, Sara. The guys were all hysterical. But James didn't stop. He kept singing and singing. He sang until his voice overpowered the team's laughter. He sang until his voice was all anyone standing in the science wing could hear.

Love,
Sophia

From: saraannblakely@gmail.com
To: ciaosoph@gmail.com
Date: September 13, 2012 at 10:09 PM
Subject: RE: James Turner

Soph—
Srry short. JA flare again. No skool 4 me 2morrow.

Fingers kill. Only gud news—dr lokz like J Timberlake.
@Coxson: Who does that?
TTYL,
Sara

From: ciaosoph@gmail.com
To: saraannblakely@gmail.com
Date: September 14, 2012 at 8:02 AM
Subject: RE: James Turner

Hey Sara,

So sorry to hear you're not feeling well again. At least you get to be examined by Hot Doc. We're in the library and I'm supposed to be researching women's suffrage for history, but I have to vent.

Last night, my Mom went on her first date (blind!) since Dad died. The guy (Albert Stevens) is a total loser. I watched him walk up to the house from my bedroom window. He claims to be a dentist but his teeth are the color of Coke when the ice melts. Seriously? And he's never been married. I mean, there's got to be something wrong with you if you're forty-something and still single, right?

He took Mom to that place in downtown Philly, Bob's Seafood, that serves oyster crackers instead of bread sticks and smells like day-old fish. Apparently, Mom says he never married because his mother got diagnosed with Parkinson's when he was twenty-eight and she's needed a lot of care over the years. Oh, and the teeth? Some medicine he took as a child stripped off the enamel. Pathetic. Albert Stevens is just one big sob story. Like some Hallmark original movie. And Mom's fallen for the whole pitiful act hook, line, and sinker— the same way she does when she sees those SPCA commercials with the sad-eyed, homeless dogs and Sarah McLachlan in the background.

The only person more disgusted with Mom than me is Nonna. She thinks James Turner is "strano" but that his smile reminds her of my Nonno. That also means he's "bello." *Hai capito?* Gotta run . . . Mrs. Wilson is eyeing me.

Love,

Sophia

From: pbrammer@gnewc.org
To: sduckett@gnewc.org
Date: September 14, 2012 at 10:01 AM
Subject: Packages?

Any sonar in those boxes? Probably too late for Salt, but they could use it on the boat in case this problem with the juveniles persists.

Best,

Peter

From: sduckett@gnewc.org
To: pbrammer@gnewc.org
Date: September 14, 2012 at 11:38 AM
Subject: RE: Packages?

Dear Peter:

Sorry, I had to clean out the staff fridge because it smelled like ass. Took the whole morning then had to go cover for the front desk for Jan, she must have Ebola or something. Jesus. So let's see. Forwarded a call to you. Some kid named James Turner worried about the whale Salt beaching and he wants you to email. About the boxes. Inside were more shells, no note or nothing this time. And no return address. I asked around about the shells. Lauren Sheridan liked the olive, guess she collects them. Went on and on about how shells are really part of the animal for protection, how their diet determines the color, blah, blah, blah. But no one here was expecting a delivery of that kind.

    —Stanley P. Duckett

From: saraannblakely@gmail.com
To: ciaosoph@gmail.com
Date: September 14, 2012 at 10:37 PM
Subject: Re: James Turner

Soph-

    Ur Mom + Albert = meh. James=*bello*? I c that if u c past *strano*.

    Cya,

    Sara

From: whaleboy4ever@gmail.com
To: the.darren.olmstead@gmail.com
Date: September 20, 2012 at 4:17 PM
Subject: Sad News

Dear Darren,

    For the past week, I'd been waiting to get a new longitude and latitude on Salt from the Greater New England Whale Conservatory. When I wasn't at school, I was chained to my email, hoping that the GNEWC scientist (we'll call him Professor Equivocator) would email me as he promised. I finally left a follow-up call for him. The voicemail message said he was out of the office. Probably on vacation.

While Professor Equivocator was sipping from a cocktail with a little umbrella in it and smearing another coat of sunscreen on his nose, the worst happened. Two days ago, Salt was found beached near Hyannis Port at approximately 3:47 p.m. EST. And how did I learn of Salt's passing, you might wonder?

By watching the six o'clock news with my parents. The television reporter didn't reveal the whale's name, but from the close-ups of his fluke, I immediately recognized the asymmetrical pattern of white spots unique to my friend's tail. The news clips showed a bunch of scientists buzzing around Salt like hungry flies, and I couldn't help but wonder whether Professor Equivocator was among them sporting a tan and vying to take home the bloated carcass for his latest study on echolocation. In one shot, Salt's small eye was still open. A couple of people took pictures with their iPhones. It was awful how Salt was being treated like some kind of freak show. (New vocabulary, more on that later.)

Of course, there was no mention of a cause of death on the news report. Because another juvenile humpback had beached in a similar spot several days before, there's always the assumption that the two were traveling in a pod and that one was sick and the other accompanied the first into the shallows where they'd be safe from predators. Personally, I think that's just a story people tell themselves to feel better—like Salt wasn't alone when he died.

A second theory has not yet been borne out by research, but I think it is the more likely cause of Salt's death. Sometimes navy sonar impairs marine mammals' echolocation, which causes problems in the animals' communications, feeding, and breeding. Whales can surface too fast trying to get away from the sonar's noise and get decompression sickness.

I couldn't make out Salt's ears to see if they were bleeding, which would have been a telltale sign. But I wouldn't doubt that some sort of human interference reset his internal clock, leading to his demise.

Anyway, regarding the use of "freak show" earlier, one thing that has become obvious to me lately is that Sam and I don't really speak the same language anymore. When Sam talks to Charlie Coxson or any of his teammates, it's like they are communicating in code. So I decided to devote an afternoon to studying the Urban Dictionary. I only got through the letter F, but immediately things started to click.

I realized I've practiced academic bulimia before tests and that my attempt at blocking a soccer ball in phys ed yesterday could only be categorized as an epic fail. So when Sam asked me which experiment we wanted to start with in Bio today, I replied, "DFW." (Which, in case you don't know, means "down for whatever.") He punched me in the arm (a little too hard) and smiled.

Speaking of the Urban Dictionary, I better go study. But I'm curious. What ended up happening with that relationship of yours?

Sincerely,
James Turner

From: the.darren.olmstead@gmail.com
To: whaleboy4ever@gmail.com
Date: September 21, 2012 at 1:28 PM
Subject: My condolences

Hey there Jamesicle,

You wanna just give me a ring and talk about all this? A voice convo might be easier.

D'air'N

From: whaleboy4ever@gmail.com
To: the.darren.olmstead@gmail.com
Date: September 21, 2012 at 3:30 PM
Subject: RE: My condolences

Hi Darren,

Thanks for the phone offer, but I'd rather stick to email. I once called a neighbor in my Italian class, Sophia Lucca, to ask about our homework. But when she answered, I forgot why I called in the first place and ended up telling her that a plant on her porch blew over. In the ensuing silence, there was this wind that was blowing in the phone receiver. Loud. I asked if she heard it. She said no. That was pretty much it. So yeah, the phone's not really my thing.

Sincerely,

James Turner

From: the.darren.olmstead@gmail.com
To: whaleboy4ever@gmail.com
Date: September 22, 2012 at 3:23 PM
Subject: RE: My condolences

Jiggity James,

I'm really sorry to hear about your buddy Salt. Do you have anyone close by you can talk to about this sort of thing? Bro or sis? Your folks? A counselor at school? Hard to tell over email how bummed you are about this, but if you're really hurting, it can help to talk to someone about it. No need to do the macho thing and hold it all inside. After my breakup—okay, dumping—I might have set some sort of record for words spoken per hour of therapy. Unfortunately, I ran out of money after four sessions, and we hadn't even made it past the time when I was six and ran into my parents' bedroom because I thought I heard my mom yelling at a burglar. That, uh, didn't turn out to be the case.

I digress, but all that to say that I'm still not quite ready to discuss the breakup. I'm not sure it'd be helpful to either of us at this time. For now I'll say this: Her name was Corinne, and I loved her.

That's crazy about the Navy subs screwing with Salt's ears. Not cool. That's the government for you. God, I sound like an old man. Feel like one too, lately.

D

From: LWoodward@OneTermLife.com
To: FHennemore@OneTermLife.com
Cc: EHale@OneTermLife.com, MRaskind@
OneTermLife.com, LEdwards@OneTermLife.com,
RShassere@OneTermLife.com, JGoettelmann@
OneTermLife.com
Date: September 22, 2012 at 4:59 PM
Subject: Golf _____, Glee _____, _____
sandwich

What goes in those blanks?

If you guessed "Donkey," you're an idiot and probably a member of Lawrence's sales team, ha! Just j.k.'ing, Law. You da Man. Fo' real.

The correct answer was "Club!"

Oh yeah! This Wednesday, we're hittin' da club, One Term Life Insurance Corp style. Hide your kids, hide your wife! (Or in Randy's case, just don't tell them!)

Anyway, I know this is supposed to be our little thing to celebrate hitting our numbers last quarter, but I was wondering if it'd be okay if I invited my roommate out with us. He's working his way through a tough breakup. And by "working through," I mean never leaving our apartment except to work, and surviving on ramen noodles and Ken Burns's *Roosevelts* documentary. He's a good dude, just needs a little kick in the ass to get himself back into society. And I believe that if there's any office in all of One Term Life Insurance Corp that can do it, it's ours.

Culver City 4eva,

Luke

From: whaleboy4ever@gmail.com
To: the.darren.olmstead@gmail.com
Date: September 22, 2012 at 11:22 PM
Subject: RE: My condolences

Dear Darren:

I've been pretty down about Salt lately. I keep listening to whale songs on CD, and I'll admit, sometimes the humpback voices are pretty ghostly sounding. I almost feel like Salt is trying to talk to me from the other side and it tears me apart.

Anyway, I guess you're right that I should talk about his death with someone, but I'm an only child. My dad is a pediatrician, and in med school he had to dissect cadavers. He still talks about this one—a six-year-old kid. My guess is that, given what he's seen, my dad wouldn't have much sympathy for a dead whale. Oh, and he's into seafood—big time. If we ever start serving whale on a bun like they do in Asia, he'll be all over it. Then there's my Mom. She'd probably send me to the school counselor, a psychiatrist, AND some kind of marine mammal grief support group. She believes in talking the way some people believe in prayer—the more you do it, the better you feel. You and Mom might get along, come to think about it. As you probably gathered from working with me on the Gabber Aid film, I don't subscribe to Mom's theory.

Anyway, I know you're busy and you've got bigger fish to fry (I actually hate that pun but I am deliriously tired and too lazy to delete) . . . Ceasing and desisting.

Sincerely,
James Turner

From: the.darren.olmstead@gmail.com
To: whaleboy4ever@gmail.com
Date: September 25, 2012 at 11: 48 PM
Subject: Fish Fry

Well, you're in luck, Whale Boy.

You wanna talk about a dead whale? Let's talk. Let's talk about anything. Because as it turns out, I decidedly do *not* have any bigger fish to fry. I don't have freakin' shrimp to fry. Don't got dang krill to fry! You know why?

My ex.

Corinne. That relationship I was talking about moving on from? Her.

The day after I last emailed you, my roomie invited me out with him and some of his work buddies. I didn't have to be in until eleven the next morning, a rare reprieve, so I said sure. If you knew the crap (can I just say "shit"? I'm saying "shit," you're 14) I go through on a daily basis, you'd understand how excited I was. I was going out on a Wednesday night! I haven't sniffed fun on a Wednesday night since I got out of school. Anyway, we went out to this dance club. Not my choice—I like to actually be able to hold a conversation at a reasonable volume when I'm socializing, call me crazy.

We arrive. Luke's buddies are a little odd, but they're nice guys. We order drinks. The place is deafeningly loud, but I'm feeling good. And life is good, as long as I ignore the bass that's thumping so hard my ears are about to bleed like poor Salt's. We're talking—yelling, rather—shooting the proverbial breeze. I'm looking around at all these pretty girls walking past, and at the packed dance floor, lights strobing over bodies, people's hands in the a-*yer* like they just don't ca-*yer*, and for the first time since Corinne and I broke up, I feel . . . shit, I'll just say it: I feel whole again. I feel like a regular person who has struggles like anyone else but is in general just going about his business, paying dues at his job, complaining about his boss. Normal, adult stuff. And as a functioning adult, albeit one with a few Jack 'n' Cokes in him, I decide what the hey, I'll hit the dance floor for a while and shake what my momma bequeathed to me. I don't know how to dance, but after seeing the bizarre convulsions of Luke's insurance company clan, I figured I'd probably look pretty decent in comparison.

So I head out there, start sidling by people to get toward the middle, and once I get there, I go all out for probably ten minutes. Just feeling it. In the zone. No room in my head for thoughts because all I can hear in there is the electronic bass drum and hi-hat going *Boom-tiss, boom-tiss, boom-tiss, boom-tiss.* All around me, there's people and their sweat and their smell. And I'm flailing to that beat: *Boom-tiss, boom-tiss, boom-tiss, boom-tiss.*

Then I open my eyes to see Corinne and her new boyfriend, right next to me on the dance floor. Corinne who supposedly hates techno. Corinne whom I would never expect to see—ever—at a dance club. She is totally oblivious, no idea that I'm there, because they're intertwined. Making out hard. So hard. Like they were both bulldogs and thought the other was a brand new bone.

Seeing her kiss someone besides me would have been heart-stompingly traumatic on its own, but the thing that's freaking me out even more, the most—what's the word?— terrifying thing about it is how little it resembled our kissing. It's like she was a different person. I know you probably have no interest in hearing this (not that that ever stops me from talking), but we almost always kissed softly. Gently. Even at our most passionate, whatever rough-and-tumble might have been happening with the rest of our bodies, we weren't lip-slammers or tongue-wrestlers. We talked about how awesome our kissing was. It was special. Sacred, I even thought. Seeing her so roughly and enthusiastically making out with this dude in a way so different from how we would have makes me feel like it wasn't that special. That the whole time, whether she knew it or not, she wanted to be kissing someone else and in some other way. So when I said and did a couple things that, no doubt, weren't the best things, rather than try to work through it she just kicked me to the curb.

At this point, watching the girl I love engage in public heavy petting, I'm out of the zone. Way out. Light-years away from the zone. The zone and I have suspended all diplomatic relations. I push a bunch of people out of the way, and the music is loud and frantic now instead of fun and exciting. The strobe light's flashing in my eyes. I fumble my way through the dance floor and head for the exit. Couldn't even hold my tears back until I got past the bouncer.

I've been lying real low ever since, Netflixin' and eating. Since you got through F in the Urban Dictionary, you'll know this one: FML.

I've been trying to remind myself (and have been getting plenty of help from my mom and my sister) that there are many fish in the sea, but it ain't helping as of now.

So feel free to drop me a line. I'm going to be streaming every documentary on Netflix until further notice.

Misery loves company,

The Old Darren and the Stream

From: Kphelps@GrainyPictureEnt.com
To: robert.pavlovik@bluescreenproductions.com
Date: September 26, 2012 at 9:49 AM
Subject: Please read carefully and absorb fully.

Remember that old Head & Shoulders shampoo commercial that said you never get a second chance to make a first impression? Well, it's true. You don't. Depending on your view, it's either ironic or appropriate that that was their slogan, because they're just the sort of advertiser that is threatening to pull their ads if we don't start getting some people to tune in, first of all, and then STAY tuned in past the commercial break. The commercial break, as you'll recall, is the sole purpose for the existence of our medium. Without it, you and I don't exist.

    The fickleness of advertisers is my problem to deal with, not yours, but I must remind you that for me to have any chance at all, I need YOU (I swore I wasn't going to resort to using all caps, but I can only restrain so much anger, though I'll try not to resort to heavy use of italics, bold print, and multiple exclamation points) to get your writers on the same page and start churning out some more stories that people can connect with. No one likes to get canceled. So don't let it happen to you. This is a three-camera Friday night family sitcom, Rob, not rocket science.

    Please don't respond to this. *JUST WRITE ME A GOOD SHOW!!!!!!!!!!!!!!!!!!!!!!!* (Sorry, but it really does feel so much better to let out that alphabetic scream.)

    Karen

From: harrietjenkins432@gmail.com
To: jolmstead@hensonacademyfl.org
Date: September 26, 2012 at 10:27 AM
Subject: RE: Introduction

Dear Coach Olmstead,

I am just now seeing this letter because there are so many emails from the school that sometimes I miss one. My name is Harriet Jenkins, mother of Michael Nguyen. I am writing because I think you made some assumptions about the kinds of people that send their kids to Henson due to you being new here. Sure, plenty of people at Henson have money, but I am a single mom who spends every dime I have to send Michael there because I want him to have a good education and be successful, which I know he can do at public school but it's so much harder there. If we lived somewhere else he would be in public school but the school we live by lost its accreditation two years ago and is a place where I think Michael would be susceptible to falling in with the wrong crowd.

I do my best to raise my son, but ain't no way I can "coach" him too. Nor would I want to, at least not the way you talk about doing it. If my son wants to stay up and play video games he's gonna do it. He's 17 years old. He needs to make decisions like that by himself. I can remind him about food too but I don't cook every meal he eats. But even if I had a rich husband and was around the house all day I wouldn't be like that with him because I think it would make him not learn to grow up.

I apologize if I sound angry, but I just want to let you know our situation is not like you seem to think it is.

Sincerely,

Harriet Jenkins

From: jolmstead@hensonacademyfl.org
To: harrietjenkins432@gmail.com
Date: September 27, 2012 at 5:48 AM
Subject: RE: Introduction

Dear Ms. Jenkins,

I'm sorry if my letter did not take into effect your circumstances. It was meant to serve as a general letter to parents and promote high expectations. As a coach I often present situations on and off the field in their ideal way, by which I mean how they would go if everything went perfect. As both a coach and a parent, I know that obviously things don't always go perfect. But I still want my players pursuing perfection even if it's sort of an impossible thing to actually get. I'm sorry I didn't make that clear in my original letter to the parents.

Irregardless, I have enjoyed working with Michael so far this season. He has a natural knack for the game, and I believe he will be a great asset as a tight end this season. He sometimes makes costly mental mistakes, but that is part of learning the game and to be expected.

Thank you for reaching out and expressing your concern,
Jack Olmstead

From: whaleboy4ever@gmail.com
To: the.darren.olmstead@gmail.com
Date: September 27, 2012 at 3:37 PM
Subject: Status Update

Dear Darren,

I don't know what to say about your situation, but I do have a movie suggestion. There's an awesome documentary,

The Whale, about an orca (hate the "killer whale" moniker)—
uplifting, friendship and rainbows kind of stuff. Maybe that
will help?

Things here are actually somewhat better. Just when I'd
resigned myself to mourning in private (more whale songs
on CD, Pop-Tarts in bed, etc.), today on the bus home, my
neighbor, Sophia Lucca, sat down next to me. Sophia and
I don't usually talk very much (recall completely awkward
phone call), but I went with my parents to her father's wake
last year. In the receiving line, I offered my condolences (only
after my mom elbowed me twice) and Sophia threw her arms
around me. Her blouse was damp from tears or sweat and I
felt her bite down on a funeral home breath mint, she was so
close. Curls loosened from her ponytail brushed my cheek. I
felt bad for getting giddy about that hug. But a hug? From a
girl not related to me? That was my first. Her mascara ruined
my best dress shirt. And you know what? I didn't really
care. She was clinging to me like I was going to save her,
and for a nanosecond, I wondered if I could. Also, it just so
happened that Sophia was unloading her books at her locker
on the awful day when Sam and the rest of the soccer team
destroyed my Biology diorama and trashed my only picture
of Salt.

But then today, there she was next to me on the bus.
Smelling like flowers and licorice and clutching her violin
case. She wanted to know if I found Salt. It didn't occur to me
at the time that she was asking about the picture the soccer
team dumped in the trash, not the actual humpback whale
himself. And so I told her the whole story: tracking the dot,
alerting the cetologist, and how my efforts were too little,
too late. He was beached. Dead. As I said that last word, she
sucked in a breath and I thought about her father, worried I'd
said too much. Man, my pulse sounded so hard in my ears,

there was no way she couldn't hear the drumming. But Sophia just said, "It's hard when you lose someone you love."

Now, I don't know much (okay, anything) about girls, but it occurs to me that what Sophia said to me on the bus today might apply to your situation with Corinne. I won't offer you any words of sympathy. You obviously cared for Corinne. What was so great about her? I'm not criticizing, believe me. I never even met Salt, and his death is eating away at me. It all just sort of makes me wonder: Is it worth it to like someone so much if there is a chance of ending up alone again anyway?

Sincerely,

James Turner

P.S. Any Netflix recommendations?

From: pbrammer@gnewc.org
To: sduckett@gnewc.org
Date: September 27, 2012 at 6:30 PM
Subject: Update

Hi Stanley:

Thanks for all of the help while I was out of the office. As expected, it's a little hard getting back in the swing of things. I never heard from my sister Elsie, even though I sent Dad's obit to her last known address, this halfway house in New York. Then I get back here and I have an email (one of 143 I received while out of the office) from a teenage kid wanting a full report on the latest loss of a young whale and a whole team in mourning about Salt, too. It's rough. I grew up in Alaska near this Inuit community. Inuit hunt whales, but they have a deep, spiritual respect for the creatures. There's this belief that the Earth is carried on the back of a whale, and the Seven Seas can fit into a whale's nostrils so that a single sneeze can cause an earthquake or flood. Any time a whale beaches, it's considered a sign that the universe is in disorder.

There's got to be something to that ancient belief because my universe, at the very least, is in disorder. Big time. But I'm trying to make some sense of it all. The shells, most of all. I talked at length to Lauren Sheridan—who, as you discovered, is an amateur conchologist. She told me that some of the shells I received in the mail are prized by collectors and might fetch good prices online if not for some little marks on their glossy exteriors. I guess the animals that live inside shells have the ability to heal from wounds to the exoskeleton, although the wounds leave scars that affect a shell's value going forward. There's the olive you received with the note that looks like it's been glazed in egg white. Then Lauren identified the other two for me as well. The one is *Pterynotus phyllopterus* or the Leafy-Winged Murex. It has more ridges than a potato chip and glows a warm yellow. The other's the *Melongena corona*, which apparently is an unusual variant of the species because a double row of spines crowns the spire. This aberration would make it attractive to a collector, even with the tiny flaw on the shell.

Thanks again for your help. And I like that new lemon stuff you used on the floor in my office. It reminds me of summer.

Best,
Peter

From: sduckett@gnewc.org
To: pbrammer@gnewc.org
Date: September 27, 2012 at 7:50 PM
Subject: RE: Update

Hi Peter,

That's a new cleaner that a friend told me about at a bike rally last weekend. Made me think of that saying, how's it go? Make lemonade out of lemons. Something like that.

—Stanley P. Duckett

From: the.darren.olmstead@gmail.com
To: whaleboy4ever@gmail.com
Date: September 27, 2012 at 8:42 PM
Subject: Netflix Recs

Hey there James Jamerson (real guy, actually, you can look him up),

Not sure what you're into as far as movies. I bet you'd dig *Whale Rider*. It's an Australian flick, I think. Check it out.

Sounds like you've got a lot on your plate, which can be good when you're dealing with loss. Keep the mind busy until the wounds heal a bit. Nobody I know died recently, thank Deity, but Corinne's absence has been rough on me. You were asking what was so great about her. I could go on for hours, but I'll try to limit myself. First off, she's a badass upright bass player in a killer bluegrass band. The girl's five foot one, the bass is six feet tall, but watching the way she owns that thing, you'd think she was playing a violin standing on end. Simply ferocious. When she lays down that bassline (I'm not opposed to bass in all situations—just not electronic bass at shuttle-launch volumes), it's like she just spread out a giant tarp, and the rest of the band just glides on top of that thing. And the whole time, she's got this determined smile on her face. Only opens her eyes once or twice a song.

Also, she laughs really hard at her own terrible jokes. This is a trait I would hate in most people, but for some reason, with her? So. Effing. Adorable.

But what I loved maybe the most was the way that girl rode in the passenger seat of a car. I'd be driving, and usually we talked like crazy, but not always, and when we weren't, you wouldn't believe the way this girl looked out the window. Like there were dangflabbin' fairies and unicorns out there. Just pure fascination with the world. Billboards, signs, people, other cars, trees, dogs, birds, freaking construction equipment. You name it. It interested her. And not in some MPDG way (Manic Pixie Dream Girl; not sure if you've made it to M in the Urban Dictionary). She *wondered* about stuff. Everything. And then came to intelligent conclusions. Excuse me for a moment while I curse aloud at my fucking stupidity for ever fucking up so badly and letting her fucking get away. Fuck.

All that to say, it was a huge bummer to see her and some other dude try to inhale each other's faces on the dance floor. Ever since, I can't stop thinking about our first kiss, which was quite a bit tamer than what I saw the other night. We'd spent the day at the beach. We kept trying to get in the water, but it was freezing, so the whole time we were in there we howled like we'd just simultaneously whacked all of our fingers with a hammer. Then we'd clamber back to our towels, joking and laughing, and that moment kept coming where our laughter died down and our bare shoulders would touch and essentially every ideal first-kiss element was in place. But I couldn't do it. We were even there at sunset! It was like a freakin' commercial for OkCupid! But I just couldn't make the move.

So I'm driving her back into the city and I can't believe what a chump I am, and I have this extended interior monologue that I won't bore you with except for the conclusion, which was something like, "If you *ever* want to be happy you're going to have to get it into your head that tomorrow is never a good time to start being the person you want to be. The time is now. And now again. And now again, until you die. At which point we *both* almost died because I was so lost in thought that I'd let the car drift toward oncoming traffic. I yanked the car back into our lane and immediately pulled over. "Are you all right?" she said.

Bam. Laid a gentle but firm kiss right on her lips. I sighed and said, "Now I am."

And of course . . . now I'm not. But I've had a lot to do at work lately, which is good. I'm actually starting to enjoy it a bit. The Show That Shall Not Be Named is still too terrible to be named, but we did an outdoor scene the other day, which almost never happens, and I got to hold the boom mic because because the boom guy had an allergy attack and was sneezing too much to keep the mic steady. Holding a boom mic is no joke. I did it on a few of my classmates' senior films, and you have to have the thing in just the right place so you're off camera but can still pick up sound. I think they appreciated that I took it seriously. Woody Allen said that ninety percent of life is showing up. Showing up and caring bumps you up a good five percent more, I'd venture. Same goes for relationships.

That's why it still kills me that I managed to bumble my way into the last five percent with Corinne. And I still haven't quite figured out why. Things were all sorts of awesome for a while. Then I felt her start to pull away. I stretched out my arms and put out my hands, but she didn't want to take them.

As far as whether it was worth it, it's hard to say. The old saying is that it's better to have loved and lost than never to have loved at all. Like that whole "many fish in the sea" thing, it sounds wise and encouraging and all that, but it doesn't really help much while you're actually going through something.

Well, c'est la vie. C'est my shitty vie.

Peace in the Entire East,

D-Dog

OCTOBER 2012

From: whaleboy4ever@gmail.com
To: the.darren.olmstead@gmail.com
Date: October 2, 2012 at 3:52 PM
Subject: RE: Netflix Recs

Dear Darren:

So I watched *Whale Rider* five times in a row marathon-style on Saturday, pausing only to nuke some ramen noodles for lunch/dinner. That's some heavy duty binge watching (Urban Dictionary, 2012) if you ask me. But a girl who saves an entire pod of beached whales by riding the largest one back into the sea like some sort of snake charmer? Unbelievable. IMO (the *Whale Rider* marathon set me back and I'm only at the I's in the Urban Dictionary), Corinne might have been your Pai.

Didn't you know how lucky you were?

As for Sophia and me, it's not what you might think. Girls aren't into me.

Yesterday, Sam sat down next to me at lunch wanting to talk. At first, I was psyched (Urban Dictionary, 2012). Sam asked me if I'd watched the latest season of *Whale Wars* on Animal Planet. Vintage Sam comment. I was pretty excited. I told him that, in my next life, I wanted to come back as conservationist (and Enemy #1 of Japanese whale poachers) Paul Watson. Then he said something about how I should do an internship on the *Sea Shepherd* someday. I said that I would have to get James Bond training somewhere first to learn how to fly a helicopter to do reconnaissance on the Japanese whale hunters like they do on *Whale Wars*. Sam nodded but his eyes were watching something over my head. And just like that, it was over. He said that he had to go, but first asked if I could put in a "good word" for him with Sophia Lucca since I'm her neighbor.

Sam's request was based on the assumption that I talk to Sophia on a regular basis. What he doesn't know and I wasn't about to tell him is that I probably talk to Mrs. D'Angelo more than to Sophia. Needless to say, I haven't had the chance to say anything to Sophia about Sam. But he is the kind of guy she would like. He's smart (especially with regards to arachnids—the kid can tell a giant house spider from a hobo spider a mile away) and he can pull off the whole Justin Bieber look thanks to his poker-straight hair. Plus, he looks legit (Urban Dictionary, 2012) in a soccer uniform and he knows a couple of cool magic tricks with a deck of cards.

Me? I like whales more than people 99 percent of the time, and I have this annoying cowlick that causes this one crazy curl to fall over my left eye (which, don't be fooled, does not make me look anything like Justin Bieber). Someday, I will do something important like discover that whale urine cures cancer, thereby saving an entire species. But right now, I am a fourteen-year-old guy whose life would make the world's most boring reality show.

Sincerely,

James Turner

From: ariannathemama@gmail.com
To: youngwidowgroup@gmail.com
Date: October 2, 2012 at 5:43 PM
Subject: Help!

Hi Ladies—

Okay, I need some advice. I've gone on a couple of dates with this guy, Albert Stevens, and I've been kind of embarrassed to talk about it in group. Stats: 45 years old, never married, no kids, dentist, medium build, dark complexion, slightly balding, bad teeth, good cheekbones, beautiful eyes with lashes as long as a fawn's. The thing is that I think I might like him.

He cultivates roses, does the Sunday crossword, and enjoys a good pinot noir. But I feel guilty like I need to go to confession or something. I still love my Peter. I do. And really, I'll never stop loving him. We would have been married 20 years this December. It's awkward after being with the same man all this time. I don't know how to do this dating thing; I've been out of the game so long. I mean, my fourteen-year-old daughter should be the one going out, not me, right?

Help!

Arianna Lucca

From: E.Crompl@gmail.com
To: youngwidowgroup@gmail.com
Date: October 2, 2012 at 6:03 PM
Subject: RE: Help!

Um, seems like you're kind of "fishin' for permission" here, Arianna, and I'm just not sure if I can give any. Just being honest. Your little girl is fourteen and she has no dad but does have 8 million hormones raging at any given moment. I just don't think it's the time. This guy doesn't exactly seem like Paul Newman, no offense, so instead of introducing this stress into your little girl's life, why not hold off until she's getting ready to move out and go to college? In the meantime, spend time with her and when she's busy, pick up one of those hobbies we've all given up over the years! (For me, it's piano. I practice for an hour three days a week now.)

    Ellen Crompton

From: MelGBerg00@hotmail.com
To: youngwidowgroup@gmail.com
Date: October 2, 2012 at 6:17 PM
Subject: RE: Help!

Yes, I agree wholeheartedly! Completely set aside your own desires for fulfillment to become a parental robot that recharges by spending *three hours* a *week* doing something *just* fun enough that you've gone years without doing it. (Ooh, if only they had sarcasm font!) Look, A and E, happy kids have happy parents. Yes, you have to be careful about bringing this man into your daughter's life, and you're going to have some complicated feelings about your late husband, and dating is, no doubt, a royal pain in the ass. But you know what, difficult and complicated things sort of come with the territory of being . . . AN ADULT!

    But that does not mean you have to be a lonely martyr. Love is for everyone, and a piano isn't a man (though I've met some pianos with a lot better personalities than some of the men I've met since Teddy passed).

    Melissa Greenberg

From: Eastwoman.Karen@gmail.com
To: youngwidowgroup@gmail.com
Date: October 2, 2012 at 8:54 PM
Subject: RE: Help!

Hi Arianna,

Um, not weighing in on either side here except on one thing. You said you "THINK you MIGHT like him." But the sentence before that you used the phrase "beautiful eyes with lashes as long as a fawn's." I'm no Sigmund Freud, but one thing's for sure, you like him! (What you do about that is your call, though.)

Karen Eastman

From: louisazstein@gmail.com
To: youngwidowgroup@gmail.com
Date: October 2, 2012 at 8:21 PM
Subject: RE: Help!

I'm not one to chime in on group emails, but I can't keep quiet. We've been talking a lot in group about the five stages of grief and how everyone moves through them at a different speed. Therefore, I don't think it is anyone's place to judge Arianna's decision to go on a couple of dates. I introduced David to my boys after our third dinner together. That's just me. I believe in being completely honest with children; they are little people after all. I didn't know then if David and I would spend the rest of our lives together. Heck, I still don't. But he's a good guy and the boys were actually relieved when he started hanging out with us on weekends. Life began to get back to normal again. We started to go to ball games, movies, water parks, synagogue, etc. as a family. My mom finally went home after a nine-month-long shiva and that was a good thing for all of us. She's the kind who would have kept the mirrors covered indefinitely.

I knew I made the right decision to let David into our lives back in June. David took us to the Devon Fair and my youngest was all smiles, holding this stuffed bear that David won for him. I could tell that something was on my LO's mind. So I asked if everything was okay. "I love Daddy," he said, "but I don't want to be sad anymore." And you know what? Neither do I.

Regards,
Louisa

From: susanjeffe@yahoo.com
To: youngwidowgroup@gmail.com
Date: October 2, 2012 at 8:37 PM
Subject: RE: Help!

Dear Arianna—

I don't know how much I have to contribute to this discussion, given that I don't have any kids. But it does occur to me from my background in psychology that introducing someone to the kids who then ends up leaving their lives at some point could reactivate their grief and contribute to an ongoing sense of instability and loss in their worlds.

Sincerely,
Susan

From: louisazstein@gmail.com
To: youngwidowgroup@gmail.com
Date: October 2, 2012 at 9:02 PM
Subject: RE: Help!

As a reminder, one of the "ground rules" of group is
non-judgment. I believe our listserv should follow the same
rules as group.

Regards,

Louisa

From: E.Crompl@gmail.com
To: youngwidowgroup@gmail.com
Date: October 2, 2012 at 6:03 PM
Subject: RE: Help!

Um, Louisa, Arianna *asked* for our opinions. Which requires
us to "judge," which everyone seems to think is a dirty word
these days, but it's not.

Ellen

From: ariannathemama@gmail.com
To: youngwidowgroup@gmail.com
Date: October 2, 2012 at 9:47 PM
Subject: RE: Help!

Hi Ladies—

Thanks for your emails. You echo some of my
own concerns.

I am, of course, very worried about my girls, but the
bigger issue might actually be my mother, believe it or not.

She lives next door to us, and she's like Napoleon in an apron, lipstick, and sensible Italian-made shoes.

To give you a little background, my mother disapproved of me leaving home before I was married, let alone moving across the state to study painting at a college where boys and girls lived in the same dorm. I think she thought I would become a *zingara*, or gypsy (her term for "hippie"). Of course, once I escaped my mother's grasp and began painting nudes at college, I didn't just associate with bohemians, but I decided to marry one—Peter Frances Lucca, an ancient-history student who wore his hair long, addressed everyone as "man," and smoked cigarettes. My mother was furious the first time I brought Peter Lucca home. The only thing that could be worse than the fact that Peter was a zingara was that he was also a third generation Sicilian. It really didn't matter that Abruzzo, the region where my mother was born, and Sicily are part of the same country; she assumed that southerners were either poor backwards farmers or slick gangsters flashing their overinflated bravado at every chance they got. "Not that I have anyting against *siciliani*," my mother once said to me, "but most turn out to be *mafiosi* or *contadini*, take your pick."

Of course, Peter turned out to be neither, and over the years, my mother slowly warmed up to him. She liked how he still made his own homemade sausages and red wine and how he respected the ancient Romans, studying their culture and marveling at how modern life, from our calendar to our use of roads, was founded on their early contributions. After Peter's wake last year, my mother even camped out in the funeral home overnight, refusing to end her vigil, even after the coffeepot ran dry and crumbs were all that remained of the tray of nutty pignoli cookies.

I share all of this for a reason. If it took my mother so long to warm up to Peter, who actually WAS Italian, what will she think of someone like Albert who is a complete nutt?

    Best,

    Arianna

From: ariannathemama@gmail.com
To: youngwidowgroup@gmail.com
Date: October 2, 2012 at 9:54 PM
Subject: Oops!

In my last email, there was a typo. I meant to write "mutt" not "nutt."

    Best,

    Arianna

From: the.darren.olmstead@gmail.com
To: whaleboy4ever@gmail.com
Date: October 4, 2012 at 7:56 PM
Subject: RE: Netflix Recs

Dear J-Turtle,

    Glad you dug *Whale Rider*. I haven't actually seen it, but I think I might now. I just guessed based on the title. Even without having seen the movie, I can safely say that Corinne was my Pai. I was a total wreck a lot of the time I was working with you in the Resource Room. Did my best to hide it, but I wasn't sleeping much at that time, and on occasion I was just downright loopy. I don't know if you remember, but this one time I showed up and I'd shaved only the left side of my face. I noticed during a trip to the bathroom. In the morning, this wasn't so bad, but my beard grows in pretty quick, so by the end of the day, I had this Jekyll-and-Hyde thing happening, which actually sort of matched my feelings at that time. The whole last hour, I was trying to creep along the wall so Mrs. Whatshername didn't notice. She asked me to check on some kid's worksheet, and I actually walked backward about ten steps to keep my right cheek facing the wall. Never forget that you've taken up correspondence with an absolute idiot.

Speaking of me being an idiot, have you been listening to anything I say about girls? If so, please stop. My advice should be considered downright dangerous. Listen to that Mrs. D'Angelo. She sounds like she's got spunk, and no one knows the secrets of women like a woman.

I won't try to give you much career advice either, other than not worrying too much about it right now. When I was your age, I wanted to be a sports writer. I imagined someday my dad, who's a high school football coach, would become the coach for a major college program, and I'd go to school there and then become their beat writer. But that was still two years before I saw *Seven Up*—the documentary, not the soda—and my life was changed forever. I don't think I've mentioned it before, but *Seven Up* is the greatest documentary series of all time. Back in the '60s, this British dude got the idea to interview a bunch of seven-year-olds about their lives.

You: "Uh, so what?"

Me: "Hold your horses there, horse-holder."

Because it turns out that the plan was they'd interview all the kids every seven years after that! Forever! Well, until they all die, I guess. And they're still doing it today! They're all the way up to *56 Up*! I mean, can you imagine? A lifelong documentary project? Documenting people becoming who they are, changing and struggling and learning. I can't imagine anything better. That's what I want to do in my documentaries.

But that's just me. I love documentaries. All I'm saying is that if there's such a thing as a whaleologist, you might want to look into that.

Or you could do like my roommate, Luke. He sells life insurance. So what, right? But we happen to live in LA, the only town where selling life insurance helps him meet women. He's a handsome dude, and everyone here's an actor, so the girls assume he is too. Then he tells them, no, he sells life insurance. And then he *really* surprises them by telling them how great it is. They're like, "What?" And he starts mentioning how he always knows he's going to have money, health insurance, etc. These girls are so used to getting hit on by aspiring actors who wait tables and make lattes that this actually sounds fascinating. He continues: "Yeah, it's really freeing knowing that in a few years I'll be able to own a house and support my family . . ." Notice how smart he is, how he keeps it vague: support his *family*. He doesn't come right out and say "support my actress wife as she navigates the incredibly uncertain and stressful waters of Hollywood," but he might as well. At this point, they always give him their number at least. It's amazing. Nice work if you can get it.

Alright, I better sign off. Another day of work awaits me.

Later,

D

P.S. Okay, I can't help myself. In answer to your question about Corinne and me, "Did you know how lucky you were?", let me offer a brief answer that should get to the heart of my feelings on the matter:

NO! NO! NOOOOOOOOOOOOOOO!!!!!!!!!!!!!!!!!!!!!!!!!!!

I had no idea how lucky I was. Not a one. Having never really been in love before, our love at first seemed like a miracle. I mean, listen to some of the things this girl said to me:

on heavy metal music: "It makes me want to not have ears."

on vegetarians: "I don't trust 'em. In a pinch, I want people
on my side who are willing to bite into some flesh."
on her boobs: "They're like roommates. We have some
good times together, but a lot of the time I just wish
they'd get out of the way so I could have some peace
and quiet."
A miracle, this girl.
But then, get this. Get the absolute insanity of *this*: I
didn't listen to the miracle. The miracle spoke to me about
problems in our relationship, needs not quite met, issues
not quite resolved—and *I didn't listen!* (Massive facepalm.
Followed by knuckle-bite. Followed by cheek-slap.)
Derpin

From: whaleboy4ever@gmail.com
To: the.darren.olmstead@gmail.com
Date: October 7, 2012 at 3:26 PM
Subject: RE: Status Update

Dear Darren:
I need to talk to you about my mom. After Salt's death,
I decided to join the American Cetacean Society and devote
some of my time to conservation efforts like sending emails to
various individuals on the International Whaling Commission
and elected officials making decisions about our seas. This, to
me, was the best way to honor Salt's memory and save others
from a similar fate.
The problem is that Mom keeps harassing me about
sitting in my bedroom in front of the computer after school.
My whale advocacy on the computer is WAY better than
playing gory video games (which is what 99 percent of my
classmates do on the computer and involves pretending to

be a sniper in Afghanistan or smashing zombies with bats).
Anyway, after the fifth day of my efforts on behalf of the
American Cetacean Society, Mom comes into my room,
sits on the edge of my bed, and tries to convince me for the
fiftieth time to join the Baking Club at school. She claims that
these brownies I made when I was five were the best she's ever
tasted. (Since then, I've done a couple tortes, some French
macaroons, worked with ganache.) Still, what Mom doesn't
know about Baking Club is: 1) I'd be the only guy in the group
(which Coxson and his gang would see as further evidence
that I am shit-for-brains or whatnot), and 2) the best part of
baking, for me, is a room so silent that you hear the flour shift
in the bowl.

So for the fiftieth time, I tell her to forget about it.
Well, she can't—no, won't—forget about it. She gives me
about thirteen other suggestions for "school and community
involvement": volunteering in a soup kitchen, trying out
for the fencing team, joining debate, blah, blah, blah. Each
suggestion is an activity she thinks I like—or WISHES I
liked. I say "no" thirteen times. She says that I can't stay at
home in my room forever. That I have to get out and interact
with people. (What does she think I do at school all day?) She
tells me that if I don't want to get more involved at school,
I have to get a job. I laugh at that suggestion. I mean, who
would hire a fourteen-year-old with no work experience
whatsoever, especially in this economy?

Well, it turns out lots of people. Mom insisted on driving
me around yesterday to Sal's Sub Shop, #1 Dry Cleaners,
Acme Grocery, and Star Arcade. All of them were accepting
applications, and somewhat reluctantly, I filled them out. No
bites yet, but I'll let you know what happens.

Sincerely,
James Turner

From: the.darren.olmstead@gmail.com
To: whaleboy4ever@gmail.com
Date: October 7, 2012 at 11:24 PM
Subject: RE: Status Update

Dear Jamesauce,

Re: your mom and her obsession with social baking, I'd pick out something she likes to do in relative privacy—fill out a crossword puzzle, watch a TV show, soak her feet—and start demanding she do it with a bunch of other people as a member of a club. See if Baking Club is so crucial then. Trust me on this one. I've made an art out of arguing with my parents.

I hope the job hunting goes well. All of those establishments you filled out job apps for sound primo. The arcade sounds like the most fun, but you always gotta eat, so slingin' subs (and getting free ones) might not be a bad racket either.

Long term, though, I wouldn't write off the whaleology thing. First of all, I'm pretty sure women dig guys who care about other living creatures besides themselves because it's actually not that common a thing. Second, I know for a *fact* that women love guys who are successful at what they do. The showrunner on The Show That Shall Not Be Named (from here on out referred to as T-S-T-S-N-B-N or "Testy Snobbin") is a dude named Rob who actually looks more like a Bob (bald spot, pot belly, and these loose, drooping–flower-petal lips), and he gets all sorts of—ahem, has much success with females. He's not good-looking, and he definitely wasn't the captain of varsity anything when he was in high school. But he's top dog, and ladies like it. (Mind you, it's a small, confused, disgruntled pack of dogs, but he's still the dominant one.)

He seems to have taken a bit of a liking to me lately because I always bring him his skinny vanilla latte from the

Corporate Coffee Shop exactly as he asks for it. What he doesn't know is that a while back I started tasting his drinks before I brought them to him and then checking out his reaction after his first sip. I would note whether he seemed to like it or not, so that after a while I learned how he liked them, and if they came out any different—too foamy, too sweet, whatever—I'd drink that one myself and order another one.

Just realized I'm a little bit proud of this. Oh, how what constitutes success has been blunted! I'm just trying to remember that it's only temporary. I will make the next *Seven Up*, but I've got to pay my dues, as they say. I'm sure the same will be true for you at wherever you end up landing a gig.

Later,

D-erring

From: whaleboy4ever@gmail.com
To: the.darren.olmstead@gmail.com
Date: October 10, 2012 at 9:45 PM
Subject: Job news

Dear Darren:

Thanks for your encouragement with regards to my career goals. It's reassuring to hear that the showrunner on Testy Snobbin, who sounds like a "late bloomer" (Mom's term for me), still has success with girls on some level. But even if that wasn't the case and my fate would be to live out the rest of my days as a lonely man eating Cheetos in front of old Jacques Cousteau reruns, I'd still become a cetologist. Judging by your moratorium on talking about Corinne, it sounds like you wouldn't be that opposed to joining me on the couch for a little *Cousteau Odyssey* marathon either. (Really, there's something for everyone in that series, even a segment on indigenous plants and animals in fresh waters if rivers are more your thing.)

As for my short-term job prospects, I have some news.

I was offered a position at Star Arcade for $8.30 an hour, and I started last Saturday. When I showed up for training, I figured that, at best, I would work the prize case for kids cashing in their Skee-Ball ticket winnings. At worst, I thought I'd be scraping hardened gum off the bottom of the Fast Wheels race car seat or unclogging the coin deposits.

Instead, I was led by this teenager with an earring in his chin (how is it even possible to pierce bone?) to a back room. Chin Piercing led me over toward jumbo stuffed animals hanging on hooks and pointed to what I thought was a white rug. "This is what you gotta wear, man," he said. He threw me the heap of white fur. When I asked him what exactly it was, he wiped his hand across his mouth, but he couldn't stop smiling.

Well, come to find out that it is an Abominable Snowman costume. In case you are like me and have no idea what an Abominable Snowman is, here is a summary of my Web research: the Abominable Snowman (also known as the yeti) is basically a bear-like creature (mythical) that lives in the Himalayas and scares the shit out of people with its height and ferocity. Anyway, it turned out I needed to wear this Abominable Snowman costume and stand on the sidewalk on King, the street that, you'll remember, every single person in our town passes on their way anywhere.

The costume smelled like cigarettes and BO And it was so big that I couldn't see out of the eye holes or breathe out of the little screened opening. I tripped twice on the way to where I thought the front door was. And I ran over a little kid (which I didn't realize until I heard the crying). I also think I pawed some girl's chest by accident. Eventually, after I'd made a complete fool out of myself, Chin Piercing grabbed my arm and escorted me out, depositing me out on the curb. I had to hold this sign that said "Abominable Gaming at Star Arcade." People beeped car horns and yelled stuff at me like, "Forget to shave?" For my entire two hour shift, I stood in the rain, contemplating running into traffic. Tomorrow is Day #2 at Star Arcade. Baking Club isn't looking so bad now.

Sincerely,

James Turner

From: pbrammer@gnewc.org
To: sduckett@gnewc.org
Date: October 15, 2012 at 12:25 PM
Subject: Shells

Dear Stanley,

Happy birthday and sorry I didn't make it down for the cake. I was caught in a horrendously long meeting with some policy makers on the benefits of creating a boat-free zone in the ocean, a sort of "whale lane," if you will.

Anyway, I just wanted to let you know that I've been racking my brain as to who could have sent me those shells and I think I've made some progress. I questioned a couple of friends from my marine biology days back at UMass and even called my ex-wife, which probably only further validated her belief that all I care about is the ocean and its related creatures.

No dice there.

Then I thought harder and came up with an entirely different hypothesis.

What if the shells came from someone else? Like maybe Elsie? What if this was her way of getting in touch with me after all these years? Maybe she's clean and she wants to reconnect and she doesn't know how. Shells were always so important to her when we were little. On vacation in Oregon, she used to bring bucketfuls home from the beach, clean them, then line them up in little rows on the outdoor porch to dry in the sun. They cluttered up her bedroom at home—it drove my mom crazy. But Elsie made these little sailor's valentines with the smallest shells, mosaics that were actually quite beautiful. I still have one that is a picture of two birds, one flying and one perched on a tree branch. Elsie wasn't much of a student, but the one thing she actually did study was her field guides and she could tell you anything you wanted to know about seashells. So all this makes me think I've got the mystery finally solved.

Anyway, I put a call in to the halfway house to see if they might know of her whereabouts. And then last night, I had this dream that I found Elsie living near the sea and she smelled like strawberry ChapStick and bath soap again like when we were little. We drank lemonade from sweaty glasses on the dunes and went for a swim. After a while, she got tired of swimming and the waves started to claw at us. A storm was churning on the horizon. I saw her go under once then twice. Her mouth formed a silent scream and the tide was strong. I'm not a strong swimmer, but somehow, Stanley, I was able to grab my sister's wrist. She struggled against me—almost fought—and it felt like she was trying to pull me under with her. I've heard that people do that when they're drowning sometimes because they panic. But I saved her.

Best,

Peter

From: sduckett@gnewc.org
To: pbrammer@gnewc.org
Date: October 17, 2012 at 3:52 PM
Subject: RE: Shells

Dear Peter,

I don't check this email as much as I should now that Jan's back. Thanks for the birthday wishes. The party at work was real nice cause when I got home I just warmed up a Hungry-Man Salisbury Steak dinner like always and watched Fox News. My mother didn't call, but she's got dementia and thinks she lives on a deserted island with Bob Barker from *The Price Is Right*. The real shitter was my dog. Dogs don't get birthdays, dumb animal didn't even sit with me on the couch.

Did you hear anything from the halfway house?

—Stanley P. Duckett

From: pbrammer@gnewc.org
To: sduckett@gnewc.org
Date: October 17, 2012 at 8:20 PM
Subject: RE: Shells

Hi Stanley—

The people at the halfway house were very hesitant at first to give me any information about my sister. There's HIPAA and client confidentiality, etc., etc. But I told them how our dad passed and Elsie's my only living relative. My voice cracked a couple of times, and I think they felt sorry for me. Anyway, the area code for the number was somewhere down in Florida.

When I got home from work today, I tried to call and some man answered. He sounded drunk or bored or both. When I asked for Elsie, he acted like I was her secret lover even though I told him multiple times I was her big brother. I tried to explain about our dad dying and the seashells arriving. Angry Guy wouldn't put her on the phone. "She don't have no brother," he finally said and then hung up. I stood there with the phone in my hand, feeling like he disconnected a vein to my heart.

Best,

Peter

From: Ktolmsteadmommy@gmail.com
To: MargaretAOlmstead@hotmail.com
Date: October 17, 2012 at 9:02 PM
Subject: Christmas

Hey Mom,

Hope things are good and that you're surviving your annual football season widowhood. Darren hadn't returned my last email so I just called him and it turned out he had a little run-in with Corinne and her new boyfriend and it kind of sent him into a tailspin. But he sounded like he was recovering. Talked a lot about work. Said he had an idea for a documentary about all these guys who work at a life insurance office. Not exactly sure why that would be interesting, but I guess that's why he's the creative one in the family. Talking to him made me miss work though.

Speaking of work, I have some unfortunate news. It doesn't look like we're going to be able to make it in for Christmas. John used up all his PTO helping me out after the twins were born and when he got sick earlier this year.

I brought up maybe just coming by myself with the kids, and it totally hurt his feelings. He said he wouldn't have minded if it wasn't their first Christmas. He's so hard to figure out sometimes. I swear, it's like he's got a condition. Random Unpredictable Sensitivity Disorder or something.

Tell Dad I said hi if you talk to him before the season's over.

Love,
Katie

From: MargaretAOlmstead@hotmail.com
To: Ktolmsteadmommy@gmail.com
Date: October 18, 2012 at 7:22 AM
Subject: RE: Christmas

Hey Katie,

It saddens me that we won't get to see you guys on Christmas, but I understand.

I was ready for football season this year. I joined a book club, and I've secretly been going to the driving range or playing nine holes at the public course a couple of times a week. Hoping I can beat your father's butt come springtime. Hopefully he won't divorce me if I do.

Yes, Darren's the creative one. That's for sure. Thank God you're practical. One dreamer child is great, but I don't know if I could handle two of them.

From: Ktolmsteadmommy@gmail.com
To: MargaretAOlmstead@hotmail.com
Date: October 18, 2012 at 12:12 PM
Subject: RE: Christmas

I think you meant that as a compliment, Mom, but I have
dreams too. Just because they don't involve Hollywood doesn't
make them not real.

    Katie

From: the.darren.olmstead@gmail.com
To: whaleboy4ever@gmail.com
Date: October 18, 2012 at 6:23 PM
Subject: RE: Job News

Dear Abominable SnowManiac,

    I must admit, the mental image of you bumbling around
like a half-sedated yeti made me LOL when I first read it,
and continues to make me SALOTI (smile and laugh on the
inside—I just made that up, BTW) each time I think of it.
Though, due to my incredibly long time in writing you back—
will get into that below—I'm sure you're an Abominable Ace
by now and are no longer running into stuff. And you've
probably cashed that first paycheck! Welcome to the rat race.
But don't worry, a surprisingly large number of cetologists got
their start as arcade mascots, so you're on the right path. (I
just made that up too.)

    My work fortunes have improved slightly as well. Rob/Bob
has been allowing me to hang out in the writers' room lately,
which is hilarious, mostly for the wrong reasons. They have
this whiteboard, but these people—*writers*, please remember—
have the worst freaking handwriting imaginable—like doctors'

scrawl on prescription pads mixed with Jackson Pollock paint splatters. So they tagged me with writing down their bullshit ideas on said board. I was actually pretty nervous and honored to do this for a couple of days, so I tried to write out exactly what they were saying, other than chopping a word or two and throwing in some useful abbrevs. I didn't want to get yelled at for messing with what they were saying.

But a couple of days ago, Rob/Bob yelled at me for writing down everything too literally. He's like, "You're not a monkey with a typewriter, Darren." To which I responded, "Thank you!" And he was like, "It's not a *blanking* compliment, *blank*-head! You're not supposed to copy out every *blankin'* word like a *blankin'* robot. You're supposed to *blankin'* paraphrase! Do you know what that word means?" And I was like, "Which one, *blankin'*?" And he goes, "No, you *blanker*! 'Paraphrase'!"

I was starting to get the sense that I was really close to getting fired, like as close as the elastic of your underwear is to your skin. So I told him I did know what "paraphrase" meant and that I would do it if that's what he wanted.

This was the first time I've really gotten chewed out at this job, but that sort of anger is actually not uncommon on set or in the writers' room. Even though the show is (supposedly) a comedy, everyone's super-tense because they're (rightfully) in constant fear of getting canceled if people stop watching the show because they realize that it's about as interesting as reading spam email backwards. It's pretty toxic in there, and everyone's always sniping at each other. I didn't want to turn into a scapegoat, so I did as he said and started trying to get at the essence of what they were saying instead of transcribing every word of their caffeine- and sugar-induced diatribes. So far, it seems like I'm doing pretty well. (Irony alert: The guy who couldn't read between the lines to save his life when it came to his ex-gf's hints is an ace at decoding the messages of a bunch of professional dorks.)

It's nothing much, but it gives me more of a sense of accomplishment than delivering the perfect latte.

How's your little Italian girl?

Please forgive my late response,

The Abominable Showman

From: mholloway@bluescreenproductions.com
To: robert.pavlovik@bluescreenproductions.com
Date: October 19, 2012 at 8:21 PM
Subject: Today's meeting

Hey Rob,

The other writers have asked me to speak for us as a group. We find your actions today both insulting and disturbing. We realize that the show is in a rough place. And I understand your desire to shake things up a little bit. But what we need is to build cohesion, and instead you've given us this silly stunt. That's all it is, nothing more. And if it blows up in our faces, we're all going to have to clean it up. Please, just tell the kid you're sorry but you just weren't thinking straight.

Marisa

From: harrietjenkins432@gmail.com
To: jolmstead@hensonacademyfl.org
Date: October 20, 2012 at 1:23 AM
Subject: Michael

Hello Coach Olmstead,

 Thank you for your response to my last email. I understand you wanting to set high standards for your players. I respect that. I just did not find some of the advice in your original letter feasible. I understand now what you were trying to do. Maybe in the future you could include language that indicates that some of the ideas presented are suggestions and not requirements. Ideals are wonderful, but when reality does not conform to them, as a parent I have to deal with the life I'm living in, if that makes sense. For example, I am an NP (nurse practitioner) and I am working a string of many nights in a row and I have found evidence that Michael has been having friends over in the evenings after I've left. He denies this, even though I am sure he is lying. I can try to take away certain privileges, but I can't really ground him because I am often not there to enforce it.

 Could you keep an eye on him at practice and please report to me if you find that he is uncooperative or unfocused? It would be much appreciated.

 Thank you for your time,
 Harriet Jenkins

From: jolmstead@hensonacademyfl.org
To: harrietjenkins432@gmail.com
Date: October 20, 2012 at 6:23 AM
Subject: RE: Michael

Dear Harriet,

Yes ma'am, I will keep an eye on him and let you know if I notice anything. He has seemed a little distracted at times lately, but so have many of the players now that their workload in class has increased.

Thanks,

Jack Olmstead

From: whaleboy4ever@gmail.com
To: the.darren.olmstead@gmail.com
Date: October 20, 2012 at 7:20 AM
Subject: RE: Job News

Dear Darren—

You had me worried when I didn't hear from you. I thought you might have overdosed on sad love songs.

Things here are fine, I guess. Sam's back in school after a bout with mono, but he's been doing the homework he missed for the past two weeks during our labs in Bio so we haven't really gotten to talk. Someone has to make sure our experiments don't spontaneously combust. Funny you should ask about Sophia Lucca. Her grandmother has been MIA and I'm down to a C in Italian; I think that she may have made a pilgrimage back to the Boot. Sophia, on the other hand . . . well, that's a story. So here it goes.

Last Saturday when I reported to work for my gig as the Abominable Snowman, I was feeling pretty shitty. The week had yielded a major setback for my cause. Several whales beached both on the coast of New England and across the pond in the UK I had to give myself a major pep talk as I suited up in the arcade's back room, because at that point, I was pretty much disgusted with the entire human race, including myself. There I was, just like the British, who turned the beached fin whales into biofuel, chasing the Almighty Dollar instead of figuring out how to save a species. (Not that I make that much. My first Star Arcade paycheck was $40.72, which my mom made me use to buy a new fleece for school.)

Anyway, as I pulled the yeti mask over my head, I realized that someone (maybe Chin Piercing, my supervisor?) had fixed the eye holes, bringing them to my height. What was he thinking? That I would actually enjoy getting to see people making fun of me in addition to just hearing it? As if to confirm my suspicion, Chin Piercing paused from counting money from the cash register long enough to smirk at me as I lumbered out to the curb with my sign.

Within the first ten minutes of standing at my post, I saw at least five kids that I recognized. One kid flicked a wad of gum at me that stuck to my fur. His buddy practically had a seizure, he was laughing so hard. Another guy took my sign and wouldn't give it back until I growled like Chewbacca. (Given that I'd never heard of a Chewbacca before, this, unfortunately, took some trial and error.)

I felt like an A.S.S.—Abominable Snow Shit.

That was the kind of day I was having when I encountered Sophia Lucca with one of her friends, Becky or Sara (all blondes look alike to me). I was sweating so hard, my hair was wet. And then Sophia's like, "He's kind of cute." Sophia steps towards me and I can smell her—all flowery with a hint of licorice just like her grandmother. She plucks the wad of gum from my fur and basically asks if she can give me a hug. A hug, man—and it didn't even take a death this time!

Before I can react, Sophia wraps her arms around me. She can probably hear my heart jackhammering away, even through the seven layers of faux fur, but at least she pretends not to notice. I drop my sign.

For that second, I'm not James. I'm an Abominable Snowman, and I put one paw on her back then the other. Of course, some jerk yells, "Get some, Bigfoot!" and Sophia blushes and bends to pick up my sign. After, Becky or Sara gives me a hug, too. All I remember about that is her elbows were pointy and her breath smelled like a sour latte. Then, just like that, it was all over.

I guess what I realized is that even the worst jobs aren't all bad all the time. It seems that's true of Testy Snobbin too.

Sincerely,

James Turner

From: the.darren.olmstead@gmail.com
To: whaleboy4ever@gmail.com
Date: October 21, 2012 at 6:56 PM
Subject: RE: Job News

Dear J to the T,

A hug! Dude, I'm envious! (Let me tell you, it's doing wonders for my self-esteem to be living vicariously through a whale-obsessed ninth grader.)

Bummer that she didn't know it was you, and that there was a mass of fur between you and her, but a hug nonetheless.

Thanks for your continuing updates on the plight of whales. I mean that. To be honest, I didn't care much about Salt or any other whales when you first started dumping

tons of information about them on me. And I thought I did
a pretty good job of showing I didn't really care, but you just
kept on writing about them, going on and on. And on. That
took spunk.

I suppose it's possible you just didn't read the cues that
I didn't give a crap. Maybe it was accidental spunk—uh,
accidental persistence, let's say—but still commendable.
You've brought me around on whales. It's amazing the crap
we humans subject them to. They seem like dang fine animals
and deserve better treatment. Glad there's people like you
looking out for them. As always, keep fighting the good fight.
Maybe I'll join you in it someday by making a cool whale doc.
I just put *The Cove* (not whales, I know) and *Blackfish* in the ol'
Netflix queue.

Fair warning, though: no matter how much you end up
helping whales, the human race will continue to disappoint
you as long as it exists. You ever thought about that saying,
"Nobody's perfect"? It's actually the key to explaining
the plight of whales and people. All right, let's start with
the premise that no one's perfect. We'll call that a given.
There's a fancy logic word for that, but I can't remember it.
Anyway, not a SINGLE PERSON alive right now on this
planet is perfect. But just for argument's sake, let's suppose
that they're really close—they're not, I'm living proof—but
let's imagine this extremely rosy scenario. Every human on
Earth is dang near perfect. Guess what, though: there are
approximately 7 BILLION of us on the planet! So if every
swell person does, say, one little shitty thing per month to
another person or to a whale or to themselves, we're already
talking about 84,000,000,000,000 (84 trillion, but I thought
it was worth seeing all the zeros) shitty things per year! And
people AREN'T all that swell. And this thought experiment
doesn't even take into account accidents, mistakes, and good

intentions that end up causing incredibly shitty outcomes!!!
(For incidents of all of these, please consult chapters 1 through
730 of *The Story of How Darren Effed It Up with Corinne*).

But all hope is not lost. Though I may be loveless, I am
not workless. Check it:

You know how I was paraphrasing all the writers' ideas
and writing them on the whiteboard? Well, the show's been
tanking pretty much all season, so ol' Rob/Bob has been
on a rampage lately. The whole writers' room is on pins
and needles waiting for his next screed, so they barely even
notice I'm there. So I started getting a little frisky with my
paraphrasing, not only *interpreting* what they said and writing
it on the board, but even trying to *improve* what they were
saying, until finally, Rob/Bob looks up on the board at the
end of a meeting and says, "Hey, who said that?" And they're
all like, "Not me." And he was all (to me), "Do you remember
who said it?" And I was all, "Well, no one said that exactly, but
Will said X, and Karen kind of proposed Y, but I figured if we
kind of took this part from X and that part of Y, then added
in another reversal where the fat, lazy dad actually teaches the
nerdy, uptight daughter something about relaxing and being
okay with who she is instead of her teaching him that he's
mostly a crappy father, which he learns in EVERY SINGLE
EFFING EPISODE IN SOME WAY OR ANOTHER,
it might be kind of cool." He says, "Cool. I like it. Darren,
guess what: you're on first." (This is Testy Snobbin speak for
"You're writing the first draft.") My draft is due at the end of
the week! Ahhh! Gotta go so I can write!

This ain't the Great American Documentary, but it's a
chance to tell a story, so I'm pretty psyched. Wish me luck.
(Really, do. I'm not just saying that.)

Signing off,

Darren

From: whaleboy4ever@gmail.com
To: the.darren.olmstead@gmail.com
Date: October 22, 2012 at 2:07 PM
Subject: RE: Job News

Darren:

Congratulations on getting picked to write the draft and good luck. That's pretty huge.

I can't remember, did I tell you that I keep having this weird dream about Salt? It starts with me and a bunch of cetologists on a research vessel. I spot Salt lobtailing near the boat and we all can tell he's in trouble because it's really shallow. The scientists try the standard technique used to save navigationally impaired cetaceans and turn on a recording of whale songs, hoping to lure Salt back out to deep waters. But he's not stupid (after all, whales have more spindle cells—the cells that control our awareness of self, right and wrong, emotional attachment, etc.—than people). Salt knows the recording isn't his pod and he cuts through the little breakers, moving toward the shore, still fascinated with the shallows. The boat is panicked and NOAA's network affiliate (the whale Coast Guard) is still 50 miles away. That's when I start singing. My vocalizations help Salt find his way to safety and deep waters. And no joke, Salt answers back, slapping his pectoral fin on the water. In the dream, it's the coolest thing, man; I totally speak Salt's language. The mutual understanding between Salt and me puzzles and amazes the other scientists, who have studied the songs for years and written lengthy papers in prestigious journals on the smallest and most insignificant discoveries. I am their hero. The Jacques Cousteau of the whale world. And I end up saving Salt's life.

Pretty cool dream, huh? You should put that in your TV

show. Psych (Urban Dictionary, 2012)! Gotta go. Kitchen timer. Pecan pie's ready.

    Sincerely,

    James Turner

From: pbrammer@gnewc.org
To: sduckett@gnewc.org
Date: October 22, 2012 at 3:45 PM
Subject: Smell

Dear Stanley:

    Even with the Blue Oceans Glade freshener I bought yesterday, my office continues to smell worse than a week-old picnic left near brackish tidewater. Do you have a moment to check the mouse trap that you put behind my desk?

    Best,

    Peter

From: sduckett@gnewc.org
To: pbrammer@gnewc.org
Date: October 22, 2012 at 4:21 PM
Subject: RE: Smell

Hi Peter:

    Not till later. Someone keeps flushing sanitary stuff down the women's commode despite the signs and now we've got a major problem. You think your office smells bad, walk by the ladies room. Only reason I'm checking this damn email instead of helping my new guy clean up the mess right now's I'm waiting to hear from the plumber.

    —Stanley P. Duckett

From: pbrammer@gnewc.org
To: sduckett@gnewc.org
Date: October 22, 2012 at 5:32 PM
Subject: Mystery Solved

Dear Stanley:

I think that the odor that I smelled in my office was coming from a rotten banana I located in the bottom drawer of my desk. So you can check that off your "to do" list. Mystery solved.

Speaking of mysteries, I finally got to speak with Elsie (after calling multiple times and hanging up when Angry Guy answered). The phone reception wasn't great because she lives on a boat docked in the Gulf with her boyfriend, who I guess she met at a Narcotics Anonymous meeting. Angry Guy's 45, so ten years older than her, never finished high school, and did time in the federal pen for armed robbery. But he's "a real peach," plays checkers, draws pen and ink landscapes, and plays the guitar. They might even get married once they save enough for a ring. Elsie talked and talked. She's seven months sober, eating vegan, practicing yoga, writing her memoir, fishing with Angry Guy, and collecting seashells to sell to nautical shops. The only time she was quiet was when I told her about Dad. They never really got along. He always hated how she called or visited just when she needed something and how the something she needed was usually money. It really got under Dad's skin and they would butt heads about her "lifestyle choices" (drug use) a lot.

Anyway, Elsie WAS the one who sent the shells. She was worried I might be mad at her for missing a couple of birthdays and Christmases. For not coming around. Somehow, any anger that I had felt toward over her the past two years (and yes, I'd definitely been mad) melted when she said she missed me and hoped I would come visit her. Before we got off the phone, she told me to give her love to Donna. I guess that's how little I said during the call. Elsie had no idea that Donna and I got divorced.

Best,

Peter

From: the.darren.olmstead@gmail.com
To: LWoodward@OneTermLife.com
Date: October 24, 2012 at 10:33 PM
Subject: I extend my hand in marriage to a piece of heated bread

Literally. But figuratively, *I propose a toast.*

To me. Yeah, I know that sounds a little cocky, but I think it's important to celebrate one's accomplishments. I just finished writing my episode for the show, and frankly, it's awesome!

So let's go out on the town tomorrow after work. Vapor Bar sound okay?

Darren

From: LWoodward@OneTermLife.com
To: the.darren.olmstead@gmail.com
Date: October 25, 2012 at 12:14 PM
Subject: RE: I extend my hand in marriage to a piece
of heated bread

First, you're a menace to the English language.

Second, I will go with you to Vapor Bar if, and only if, you take your laundry out of the dryer before we leave so I can do mine. If this sounds familiar it's because I've been telling you this for the past week.

Congrats on the writing,

Luke

From: the.darren.olmstead@gmail.com
To: whaleboy4ever@gmail.com
Date: October 26, 2012 at 9:49 PM
Subject: RE: Job News

Dear James:

Oh, how the people who briefly thought they might just be a little mighty have fallen.

As I mentioned before, Rob/Bob and the others showed some appreciation when I enlightened them to the fact that not every episode of the show had to end in the same way.

But it appears I considered this praise to be a bit more of a mandate for change than it really was. You could argue that I should have seen this coming, because the outline they gave me to write the episode had all the same old boring tropes. They basically wanted me to just color it in, paint by numbers. But I was feeling all inspired, you know? I took that thing and made it my own! I put my own personal stamp on it!

Well, turns out they liked a LITTLE bit of a change, but they weren't ready to handle the radical reformation I presented in my episode. To demonstrate why they didn't like it, and why I'm no longer invited to the writers' room and am back on coffee-and-copies duty, and why Rob/Bob has been giving me the stink-eye for the last week, and why I'm considering looking into an Abominable Snowman gig, let us A-B a typical Testy Snobbin episode with mine.

Episode 6 from last season: In the first scene, Reasonable Mom, already annoyed because she has decided today is the day she must put away all her summer clothes and get out her winter ones, nags Bumbling Dad about the high water bill, which she insists is the result of the constantly running toilet, which Bumbling Dad promises to fix this weekend. Bumbling Dad (henceforth BuD) is watching college football and doesn't want to hear it. Reasonable Mom (henceforth ReMo) leaves in a huff. Just before the first commercial break, as BuD happily watches football, a pipe bursts, seemingly because of the ignored toilet issues (this isn't explained), and the television short-circuits because water gets in the fuse box or something (this isn't explained), and BuD is unable to watch the game. He calls a plumber friend, who of course, is watching the game, and they end up watching the game at the plumber's house instead of fixing the toilet, convinced they can do it afterward. But then the game goes into overtime. Then double overtime. Then triple overtime. And so on.

Meanwhile, ReMo is at home freaking out, and eventually calls this emergency plumber who comes over and charges them a jillion bucks to fix the pipe. There goes their vacation money. BuD slightly redeems himself at the end with a desperate and heartfelt apology and by putting away all of ReMo's summer clothes, getting out her winter ones, and creating a color-coded system denoting the boxes in the attic where he put all the summer clothes, so it'll be easier for her to find them. Because BuD tracks inventory at a warehouse, organization is one of his relative strengths and one of ReMo's minor flaws. She's touched by his effort and thanks him. He apologizes for all the trouble he caused. They kiss. He makes a little remark implying he might get lucky that night, and she rebuffs him with equal parts snark and gentleness. And . . . scene.

There's also a subplot involving Type A Daughter (TAD) and Rambunctious Teenage Son (RaTS) in which TAD and RaTS run for student council against each other. In the end, they agree to be co-councilpeople or some other cornier-than-Fritos bullshit.

Confident of the superiority of my script to the above load of junk, I stopped in the Corporate Coffee Shop as usual on the morning we were going to discuss the script. Even though I've been getting to hang out and act like a writer, I was still on latte duty for ol' Rob/Bob. Since it's fall, R/B has switched over to pumpkin-spice lattes. This is what people in southern California do to conjure the changing leaves and brisk temperatures that people in the rest of the country get in autumn, since we don't really have seasons out here. R/B's originally from Chicago, a place with real fall, which is why I think he's extra-sensitive about these pumpkin-spice lattes. It took me a week of pre-sipping before delivery then careful examination of his facial expressions to really figure out how he liked them. I chatted with my usual barista, and I was so excited about my script that I almost told her the name of the show I worked on. She's definitely a cutie, a fact that I had somehow ignored in all these previous months of pining for Corinne.

Anyway, just before the meeting I walked into his office, handed him his latte, and waited for his reaction. Usually he's typing like mad on his laptop, and he just silently grabs the latte and starts sipping while, amazingly, continuing to type with the other hand. But this time, he paused and gave me this really expectant look, like he was waiting for me to say something, so I said, "Mornin', Rob."

And he said, "Hey Darren, how you doing?" Now this doesn't sound like much, but in the almost year I've been working there, never has ol' R/B inquired about me in any way. I was a bit stunned, and I didn't know what to say. "Have a seat," R/B said.

I did. He just stared at me, one of his cheeks twitching every couple of seconds, which pulled his big droopy lips to the side like he was a cow chewing cud at hyper speed. "So, listen, this was a bit of an experiment, letting a PA with no experience take a crack at an episode."

"Well," I said, "thanks for taking the risk on me."

Just then Rob's phone started ringing. He glanced at the caller ID and bit down on his bottom lip so hard I'm surprised he didn't draw blood. He put up a finger to tell me to wait. He put the phone up by his ear but not right on it like the thing smelled bad or something. "Hi, Karen," he muttered. Karen is one of the studio execs.

The sound that came through the other end of that phone in response was one of the eeriest things I've ever heard, a primal, rabid, downright Chewbacca-like yell that lasted about ten seconds. During the last three or so of those seconds, R/B was waving at me to get out of his office.

So even though we didn't get to talk, I was feeling good that I'd been given a private audience with the showrunner. It seemed like we were about to have a man-to-man conversation. I figured he was about to tell me how fresh my idea was ("You're raw but you've got talent, kid"), how it broke the show's pattern of creating contrived conflicts that can be resolved in one fell swoop just before the closing credits play, as if that's how life works. You see, the premise of my script (Season 3, episode 8) was that BuD wakes up in the morning, inexplicably, as a beached humpback whale. I share the blame, uh, I mean credit, with you, on him being a HBW. It's sort of immaterial, though; the point was that he had to be something lonely, pitiable, and in need of help. Since he's BuD, though, he's too macho and embarrassed to ask for help getting off the beach. The point of my episode was that BuD was finally going to have the existential crisis that his repetitive, meaningless life demanded, and he would either triumph or fail, and the show (and television as we know it, I figured) would be changed forever either way. I hadn't quite figured out the whole triumph v. fail thing though, so it ended with a "To Be Continued . . ."

I really thought it was good. I still think it might be good. So that's why it hurt especially bad when he completely demolished what I wrote in the writers' meeting an hour later. I mean, I've been yelled at plenty of times (see: dad, my), even a couple times in front of other people, but it was like Rob/ Bob had turned into one of those celebrity chefs or something, he was yelling and cursing so much. And even though he kept yelling at me, it was like he was yelling to the other writers. They were the television audience watching at home and needing to be convinced to keep watching, and I was just a prop, not even a person.

Long story short, they had to run one of those memory episodes where they come up with a frame story and then run clips from old shows to fill the half hour, and I'm coffee-and-copies guy again.

Best of luck in work and love.

To Be Continued . . .

Daring

From: robert.pavlovik@bluescreenproductions.com
To: mholloway@bluescreenproductions.com
Date: October 27, 2012 at 10: 45 PM
Subject: RE: meeting today

Hey M,

Writing to save you the trouble of having to say "I told you so." I knew the kid wasn't ready, but I needed a sacrificial lamb, and he was just right there. Please don't tell the rest of the gang I said that. I'll apologize to them in person. Not sure what I was thinking. Might have had something to do with this football coach I had back in high school. I was a linebacker, believe it or not. One game, we were losing to some team we should have been creaming, and he pulled me and the other two best players on defense out and put in these three total scrubs for the first series of the second half. We ate our humble pie, watched the other team march down and score again, and put our helmets back on to come in. He sat us right back down. We didn't get in the rest of the game and we got absolutely creamed. But I tell you what, that was the last game we lost until the state semis, because the other guys and I were so mad that we worked our butts off for the rest of the season just to spite our coach for doing that to us.

How have you been otherwise? I see work-you every day, but I miss seeing other-you, the you with her fingers running through my chest hair. I'm not saying that to try to change anything. I know that's not possible. Just saying it because it's true. I hope Ron and the kids are good.

Rob

From: mholloway@bluescreenproductions.com
To: robert.pavlovik@bluescreenproductions.com
Date: October 27, 2012 at 11:37 PM
Subject: RE: meeting today

Not sure what it says about you that you think the techniques that motivated you as a teenage jock would be effective with a bunch of adult professionals.

Kids are fine. Ron and I are in counseling.

From: jolmstead@hensonacademyfl.org
To: harrietjenkins432@gmail.com
Date: October 28, 2012 at 5: 48 AM
Subject: RE: Michael

Dear Harriet,

I am writing to ask about Michael's recent absence. Missing practice (and school) at this time of year can be quite detrimental. Is he feeling any better? None of the other players seem to have talked to him. Please let me know if everything's all right. If it's the flu or something like that, please let me know, as this information may affect game-planning in the coming days. I was going to email you soon anyway because Michael seemed especially distracted last week in practice and Friday's game. Coach Erickson and I have been riding him pretty hard for a while, but he still seems to be having trouble keeping his head in the game.

We could really use Michael in this Friday's game.

Thanks,

Jack Olmstead

From: harrietjenkins432@gmail.com
To: jolmstead@hensonacademyfl.org
Date: October 28, 2012 at 3:48 PM
Subject: RE: Michael

Dear Coach Olmstead,

Michael will be back at school tomorrow. He has not been ill. Rather, he had a run-in with the law that we have been dealing with. It happened when he was in Tampa over the fall break a couple weeks ago. I would rather not discuss details and would rather you didn't share details of the incident with the administration (it's probably a matter of public record if you would like to look it up), but I will say that although Michael was far from innocent in this situation, he's the only one who got in trouble because he was trying to protect his friends who were far more involved with the wrongdoing. A couple of those friends are on the football team, by the way. Please discipline Michael as you see fit. If you would like the names of the other players involved, please let me know.

Sincerely,

Harriet James

From: jolmstead@hensonacademyfl.org
To: harrietjenkins432@gmail.com
Date: October 29, 2012 at 6:02 AM
Subject: RE: Michael

Harriet,

I will speak to Michael and come up with an appropriate punishment for all involved.

Jack Olmstead

From: whaleboy4ever@gmail.com
To: the.darren.olmstead@gmail.com
Date: October 30, 2012 at 5:32 PM
Subject: RE: Job News

Dear Darren:

Sorry to hear about your work situation and for not writing sooner. Work's been keeping me busy. They gave me more hours, which I hated at first. Less time researching whales or hanging out in the kitchen, baking and stuff. Not to mention, every minute of every shift, I was waiting for people to harass me: steal my sign, throw gum in my fur, shout obscenities at me. I was so on edge that it felt like being at school. But worse. Then I realized that no one actually knew that it was me in the costume, and—if I really thought about it—the majority of people walking by didn't tease me at all. Just the opposite. Kids waved at me, upperclassmen gave me high fives, an old lady (who might have had dementia) asked for my autograph.

Now, I kind of like being the Abominable Snowman. (Plus, the costume adds about six inches to my actual height and a lot more bulk than I'd ever have in real life—even if I actually used the Jillian Michaels *Biggest Loser* free weights under my bed that my Dad bought me two years ago.) Kids, teens, housewives, businessmen—people passing by—talk to me, and so I talk back (in a slightly altered version of my voice). I'm surprised by what comes out: funny stories I make up about life as a yeti and slang I've learned in the Urban Dictionary. I can do stuff as an Abominable Snowman that I can't do in real life. Like cartwheel, speak in Pig Latin, stand on my head, and yodel. It is insane.

That's not to say that things aren't still kind of rough. I have A LOT of time for my mind to wander at work, and most of the time, I'm thinking about Salt. Today, I imagined his last swim—algae blossoming around him and plankton riding the ocean's currents. A school of fish darting in and out of the sea grass. His lone shadow, dark against the sand. He calls out to his pod and journeys toward shallow waters alone. His own air bubbles form a little net around him. Maybe he's kind of lost in the silence. Or in the way his silvery body creates its own solitary wake.

    Sincerely,

    James Turner

From: the.darren.olmstead@gmail.com
To: whaleboy4ever@gmail.com
Date: October 31, 2012 at 1:25 AM
Subject: RE: Job News

Dear Jimmy,

    Dang, dog. You're quite the whale poet. You should meet my buddy Sash. He writes poems about stuff way weirder than whales.

    Congrats on your successes in work and socializing. I'm doing better in the latter than the former. Soon after they dissed my Kafkaesque existential crisis whale plot, I sort of had my own Kafkaesque existential crisis. I started thinking about ending up like Rob/Bob years down the line and all the crap I'd have to go through just to get to that point, and one day Rob/Bob told me he wanted a pumpkin-spice latte, so I got him one, and when I brought it to him he didn't like it, so he made me go to a different coffee shop to get another one. As I returned to the studio, it was as if the warm cup in my hands and the smell of the pumpkin spice and cinnamon awakened my soul (thank you, Corporate Coffee Shop people!). I realized that this is not what my life is supposed to be. Bringing coffee to Rob/Bob et al is a fine job if one day you want to be him. But I don't! I really don't! I want to make cool documentaries for cool people, not moronic sitcoms for the masses where everything gets neatly tied up in the last few minutes of every episode and everyone kisses and makes up like it's nothing and then does it all over again next week. So the next day I quit. I even dropped the "moronic sitcoms for the masses" line on Rob/Bob as I did. It felt pretty good.

However, this news was not received well by my dad. He responded like a football coach berating his team at halftime of a big game. I'm pretty sure he was madder at me than he's ever been at one of his players, though, because no matter how dumb a thing his player did, or how lazy he was during practice, he hadn't spent **EIGHTY THOUSAND DOLLARS** (the bold caps are meant to communicate that my dad yelled every time he mentioned this figure) sending the player to tackling school or whatever. However, that's how much he spent on my college education—which I thanked him for repeatedly during this conversation, but he didn't seem too appreciative of my appreciation at that moment. He goes, "When opportunity knocks, you invite him in and show him your best stuff! You don't ignore the doorbell because you're sitting on the couch smoking pot with your friends!"

And I'm like, "Wait, I'm confused, does opportunity ring or knock? I want to know so I can be prepared."

"Don't be a smart-ass!"

"Fair enough, but what are you even talking about? I don't smoke pot."

"It's just an example," he says. "My point is that if you don't answer the door because you're stoned or you think you're too big for your britches, opportunity might just hop on back in the car and go somewhere else!"

I was this close to asking him what sort of car Opportunity drives so I could look out for it, but I knew this would have been a bad idea. And as weird as his metaphor was, I got his point. The thing is, he sees me quitting Testy Snobbin as me flushing those 80 Gs he spent down the toilet, whereas I saw Testy Snobbin as an insult to the education paid for by that money. Anyway, this is how it always works with us. We'll go a few weeks without speaking and then it'll all be fine. Luckily my mom was more supportive because she's my mom and that's how she rolls.

My roommate Luke keeps saying he could get me a job at the insurance company, but I'm just not sure if I could handle it. Apparently they have these sales meetings that last for hours where they try to get everyone fired up about selling and being a team, and they sound horrific. Cheering, raffles, company-made videos that make fun of the other insurance companies. A gauntlet of high-fiving, fist-bumping, backslapping teammates. The whole thing sounds really creepy. Luke pretty much admits that it is, but he sees it as just part of life's necessary crap. I *sort* of get this, since almost everyone who makes movies has to do things like what I did at Testy Snobbin in order to get experience and meet the right people. But it's all in service of getting to that pot of gold eventually—a chance to make a movie or a show. The reward for selling insurance, seems to me, would be retiring so you don't have to sell any more insurance. But I shouldn't criticize. After all, he's the one with a car that has working air-conditioning and for whom mac 'n' cheese is a side dish instead of a thrice-weekly main course. We'll see.

Take care,

Darren

From: gigifullnothalfnelson90@hotmail.com
To: mtbaker@melissatbakerdesigns.com
Date: October 31, 2012 at 11:42 AM
Subject: You!

Greetings and happy Scary/Sexy Costume Day, Melissa T.,

What's shaking? Those new purses flying off the shelf? So proud of you for going all in on this (though it sux dux how friggin' busy you are now!). I'm not insulted, though. I swear. (Sniffles, holds back tears.) But no, seriously, it's awesome. I don't think I'll ever go beyond my little Etsy page. Not a boss like you.

ErMahGerd, terrible news. My cute little latte-sipper stopped coming in. He was always kind of throwing it out there that he worked in TV but never mentioned what show, and I could tell he wanted me to ask which show but I wouldn't. (You wanna flirt with me, you make the small talk, I always say.) But the funny part was that he was always saying his boss was this total hard-ass about everything so that's why he had to taste-test the lattes, but if the boss ever found out he'd totally get fired. So I'm wondering if the boss found out he'd been sampling or, even worse, he FORGOT to sample the pumpkin spice latte I made him the other day and he totally got fired because of my latte skills. Oh, the guilt!

Let's get drinkies this w/e or we're not best friends anymore, 'kay?

Gigi

From: mtbaker@melissatbakerdesigns.com
To: gigifullnothalfnelson90@hotmail.com
Date: October 31, 2012 at 5:25 PM
Subject: RE: You!

Hey Gigi!

Business is BOOMing over here. The bananas have been hitting the fan for like two weeks straight.

So YES, let's get together this weekend. Date with Tripp Friday but free Saturday. (Things have been a teensy bit weird with us lately. Must discuss.) Lemme know if that works.

Shame about the yappy latte cutie. But I'm sure he won't be the last showbiz guy to darken the door of your little beanery.

C U soon,

Mel

NOVEMBER 2012

From: saraannblakely@gmail.com
To: ciaosoph@gmail.com
Date: November 1, 2012 at 10:14 AM
Subject: After skool

In stdy hall, bord. Gud view tho . . . Sam Pick. Story: I
bumped into Sam @ locker & he noticed my new haircut
("lokz nice") then he
    Srry hurts 2 much 2 finish. Can u hang out after skool w/
me & Becky? Tell u then.
    XO,
    Sara

From: ciaosoph@gmail.com
To: saraannblakely@gmail.com
Date: November 2, 2012 at 9:07 PM
Subject: Sorry!!

Hey Sara,
    Sorry! I just got your email. Nonna just got back from

Italy and she insisted that I go to the cemetery for Il Giorno dei Morti, a holiday I didn't even know existed. My sister was at choir practice (lucky) and Mom had another date with Albert (gag). So I was the only one around and it's hard to avoid Nonna when she lives next door. Even though I'd rather have done anything else, even Bio homework, Nonna offered me no choice and so we lugged her shopping bags to the bus stop outside of our subdivision. No one I know other than Nonna takes the green Pace buses, and now I know why. Everyone on the bus had either gray hair, a walker, or both. Let's just say I now know the medical histories of every old woman in our ZIP code.

Anyway, the bus let us off in front of Saint Cecilia's and then we hiked back toward the cemetery. The last time I was back there was to bury Dad. We didn't even go to Dad's grave on the one-year anniversary of his death. Instead, Mom decided we should honor Dad's memory by doing something he loved. So Mom, Anna Maria, and I spent that afternoon looking at ancient Egyptian artifacts in Dad's favorite wing of the Philadelphia Museum of Art. Mom even tried to imitate Dad's Rocky Balboa impression by running up the museum's front steps. But she ended up tripping and spraining her ankle. After, we drove to Chinatown and ate at the Three Happiness Restaurant near Temple where Dad used to teach. (Have you ever gone? Their sweet and sour pork is sooooo good.) The waiters, out of habit, left the usual four fortune cookies instead of three when they brought the bill.

So I haven't been to the cemetery in a while. Nonna seemed to feel at home there today. She just approached Dad's stone and kissed it. And even though I wanted to believe that Dad was anywhere but there, under that stone in that colorless field, I touched my lips to the marble too.

After a few prayers, Nonna Rita sprinkled Dad's grave

with a little bottle of holy water. She told me that it's Italian tradition to clean ancestors' grave sites on All Souls' Day (who knew?) and so we got to work because it was starting to get dark. While Nonna weeded, I planted the mums she bought. All of them yellow, Dad's favorite color. The next part was pretty weird. Nonna Rita spread down a blanket from one of the shopping bags. She pulled out a tin of these hard cookies called "bones of the dead" and poured paper cups full of wine for Dad and her deceased family members in Italy.

Thank God no one saw us. What did you guys end up doing? Please don't tell me that you went to Forever 21 and got those matching sweaters without me.

Love,

Soph

From: saraannblakely@gmail.com
To: ciaosoph@gmail.com
Date: November 2, 2012 at 9:35 PM
Subject: RE: Sorry!

Hey Soph-

U didn't miss anything b/c 4got bout PT appt.

Apparently, ppl w/ JA don't have social lives. I c dr. > I c bestie.

Srry bout ur dad. Rmr how he let us stay up L8 @ camp & eat marshmallows? Gud man.

Life sux.

C U,

Sara

P.S. Found right color foundation 2 cover rash frm l8est flare. :)

From: whaleboy4ever@gmail.com
To: the.darren.olmstead@gmail.com
Date: November 17, 2012 at 4:31 PM
Subject: Party

Dear Darren,

Craziness is happening here. I have to type fast because I'm using Chin Piercing's computer while he's on break. Anyway, like an hour ago, Coxson, Sam, and the rest of the soccer guys walked toward me from the arcade parking lot. Here's how it went down:

Coxson: "What's shaking, Snowdude?"

(My throat started tightening the way it does at school whenever I see him. The noise that came out resembled a snort, I guess.)

Coxson: "What the hell was that?"

(I could tell that he was choosing from his vast stores of insults for the best way to make fun of me. The thing is that, as the Abominable Snowman, I am actually taller than Coxson. And somehow—don't ask me how—that helped me conjure up the following response.)

Me: "A huge hairball."

Coxson: "Funny. You're funny, Snowdude."

To make a long story short, for the next fifteen minutes, I told the guys some of my yeti jokes. And then we tried to see who can do the best Chewbacca (thanks to YouTube I now know who he is). Sam's impersonation was ridiculously high-pitched and Charlie said he sounded like a girl. My Chewbacca was the best, at least according to Charlie. He fist-bumped me and invited me to Smith's party right after my shift.

I think Sam was trying to redeem himself after the Chewbacca fail because he went, "But the invite only stands if you wear the Snowdude duds."

To which I replied, "What else would I wear?"

All of this to say that in approximately forty-eight minutes, I am going to my first ever high school party dressed as an Abominable Snowman.

Sincerely,

James Turner

From: the.darren.olmstead@gmail.com
To: whaleboy4ever@gmail.com
Date: November 17, 2012 at 5:05 PM
Subject: RE: Party

Dear James,

I should complete my LinkedIn profile. But before I do, I want to check in on your going as Snowdude to this party. I'm glad you feel comfortable talking to people when you wear it. Whatever works. Remember, though, it will be a lot hotter inside someone's house than standing outside in November. Wear deodorant. Lots of it. It'd be a shame to get ostracized from a party simply because you're covered in your own funk. It'd be even more of a shame if your name lent itself nicely to a little nickname, say BODO—short for Body Odor Darren Olmstead, for example—that ended up sticking with you for like a year after the infamous party at which you stunk up the joint because you'd timed your workout for just before the party so you'd still be a little swole when you got there and the girls would be like "daaaaaaayummm," but then you lost track of time and next thing you knew your ride was in the driveway honking the horn and you decided "what the hey" and just went to the party sans showering.

Good luck!

Baron Von Darren

From: harrietjenkins432@gmail.com
To: jolmstead@hensonacademyfl.org
Date: November 18, 2012 at 4:00 PM
Subject: Thank You

Dear Coach O,

    I just wanted to thank you for all you did for Michael this season, and particularly for the play at the end of the game. I don't know if Michael can appreciate it right now, especially with all the other stuff he's dealing with at the moment, but some day he will be very grateful to you for giving him the opportunity.

    Sincerely,

    Harriet Jenkins

From: jolmstead@hensonacademyfl.org
To: harrietjenkins432@gmail.com
Date: November 19, 2012 at 3:45 AM
Subject: RE: Thank You

Hello Harriet,

    Thanks for the kind words. It was a pleasure to coach Michael. As far as how he feels about the play against McDowell, it would be great if he ended up feeling thankful, but I would not blame him if he never did.

From: sduckett@gnewc.org
To: pbrammer@gnewc.org
Date: November 22, 2012 at 7:35 PM
Subject: Thanksgiving

Hi Peter,

Happy Thanksgiving. I just finished my Hungry Man and turned on the tube. I watched football all day and lost my voice yelling at Andy Reid so I was cruising and there was this TV show on called *Intervention*. Made me think of you. Any news on your sister?

—Stanley P. Duckett

From: pbrammer@gnewc.org
To: sduckett@gnewc.org
Date: November 22, 2012 at 9:46 PM
Subject: RE: Thanksgiving

Happy Thanksgiving to you, Stanley. Sounds like your day was slightly more eventful than mine. I have never really followed the Eagles or football but I'd wager that it is probably more interesting than solitaire. After my 14th game, I heated up this frozen casserole that I found in my dad's freezer when I cleared out the apartment. The label was in my mom's handwriting and she used to be a killer chef, but she passed away almost a year before my dad. Needless to say, the casserole tasted a little stale.

Thanks for asking about Elsie. We talked on the phone today. She was making a Tofurky for the holiday and then I guess tomorrow she and Angry Guy are going to the Keys for a little vacation and to shell. I guess that kind of thing is easy to do when your house is also a boat. There is a plan in place for me to visit, but Elsie hasn't been able to commit to a date.

Regarding *Intervention*, I've experienced enough holidays-turned-interventions with my sister, so I stay away from those TV shows about addicts; I find they're misleading. One Christmas, my sister actually threw an entire turkey at my father's head when he confronted her on stealing 20 bucks from his wallet, as my apron-clad mother (who just spent hours preparing said bird) wailed in the background. To this day, I can't eat turkey without feeling sick to my stomach. Here's the thing about real life interventions: no matter how uncomfortable things get, you can't change the channel.

Best,

Peter

DECEMBER 2012

From: whaleboy4ever@gmail.com
To: the.darren.olmstead@gmail.com
Date: December 6, 2012 at 4:56 PM
Subject: RE: Party

Dear D-Dog:

Sorry about the lag time in my response. Had to work double shifts over the holiday because we were busy with the schools out for Thanksgiving.

Anyway, I'm guessing that you want to know how the party went. I had to wait for the guys to pick me up on King St. Given that's my normal habitat, no one thought it strange for me to be standing there pacing back and forth. I took your advice about deodorant and bought a stick at the 7-Eleven. Clinical-strength stuff. Don't know how well it worked though. My hair was soaked before Coxson's car even pulled up.

For the most part, the ride to Smith's was uneventful. It was Coxson, Sam, and some other kid I don't know that well. The guys talked about previous "party fouls." Most involved Sam. Allegedly, Sam once peed in some kid's mother's flower

pot. At one point, Charlie ashed out the window. The ash
flew through my window and onto my lap, singeing my fur
pretty bad. I knew Chin Piercing would have a shit fit (Urban
Dictionary, 2012) when he saw the damage. But I was lucky.
The whole costume probably could have gone up in flames.
Then Charlie offered me a cigarette. I refused, saying I wasn't
into the whole yellow teeth look he had going on. Sam and the
other kid in the car thought that was hilarious. Charlie—not
so much. He gave me the same look in the rearview mirror
that he'd given some guy earlier who'd flipped him the bird.

Anyway, I'd never been to Craig Smith's before, but it
wasn't hard to tell which house it was. Cars were everywhere.
Inside, people were clutching beer bottles and red cups filled
with something called jungle juice, which sounded like a drink
that an Abominable Snowman would like. Smith poured me a
cup. Wearing the yeti costume meant sweating and sweating
meant I was thirsty, but I couldn't drink with my Abominable
head on so I went to the powder room and guzzled the juice in
one long swallow. I knew that there was alcohol in there, but it
was so sweet and good.

More to come. If I don't start this Biology assignment on
cellular respiration, I'll bring down my average to an "A–."

Keeping it real,

J-Wow

From: the.darren.olmstead@gmail.com
To: whaleboy4ever@gmail.com
Date: December 9, 2012 at 5:35 PM
Subject: RE: Party

Dear Jamesicle,

You master of suspense! You're like the Hitchcock of

email stories! Stopping right before things were gonna get nuts, dropping that big ol' cliffhanger on me! I'm hanging on a cliff here, and the muscles in my fingers and forearm are burning! The mind races: After imbibing the juice of the jungle (BTW, jungle juice has been around since approximately the Middle Ages and has been passed down through countless generations of inexperienced drinkers), what became of our furry and freshly inebriated hero? Will he suffer the same fate as his email confidante did at his first drinking party, vomiting so profusely all over the host's kitchen counter and dinner table and couch and dog that the host freaked out and called the paramedics? Or will he soar through the jungle (juice) like Tarzan? There's no telling.

Well played, you little scamp!

Waiting on pins and needles (and trying not to feel like a complete dork because my life is vastly less interesting than yours),

Darren Starin'

From: whaleboy4ever@gmail.com
To: the.darren.olmstead@gmail.com
Date: December 14, 2012 at 8:25 PM
Subject: RE: Party

Dear D-Dogg,

My sincerest apologies for the long silence again. As you might surmise, winter is the Abominable Snowdude's busy season and I've been swamped with overtime at work.

Basically, from where I left off, I guzzle the juice in about two seconds flat then plop the yeti head back on, leave the bathroom, and rejoin the party. I almost forget I'm James Turner. Almost. One glance in the general direction of my

Chuck Taylors helps me remember that I have size 14 paws for feet.

Coxson wants me to retell this joke that I supposedly told during the car ride to the party. The problem is that I can't even remember the punch line and my tongue feels like it weighs two tons (just like a humpback's). I'm sweating and trying to recall what I said that was even remotely cool or interesting. I grab for the easiest thing: whales. Just as I'm about to spout some random fact about the social lives of male humpbacks, I suddenly feel seven feet tall. (That's my height for real in the yeti costume.) I deliver a punch line, something to do with the size of my (snow)balls. The guys roar and invite me to join them in a game.

Are you familiar with Seven Minutes in Heaven? Well, I wasn't.

We had to draw a colored paper with a girl's name on it from a baseball cap. Another jungle juice or two later, and it's my turn. With the paws, it's kind of hard to open the paper to see the name. Everyone thinks that's pretty hilarious. Eventually, Sam helps me. When he announces the name, I swear I see his shoulders droop a bit. And that's how I end up in a dark closet with Sophia Lucca, which might just be better than swimming with a humpback. From watching other couples disappear behind the door, I get the gist of what's supposed to happen in there. Once we're inside, the closet smells like rainy days and there's no place to sit except on a pile of old board games. Sophia leans her head against the door and a piece of gum gets stuck in her hair. Once we get the gum situation under control, all Sophia wants to do is talk. Which would be fine except that what she wants to talk about is my least favorite subject.

Me.

She wants to know my real identity.

She makes a bunch of guesses, including Robert Flemming, who almost died choking on a mouthful of marshmallows during this game called Chubby Bunny in eighth grade. The one minute warning comes from the people outside. I am feeling confused and happy, lost and safe. And I pull off the Abominable Snowman head.

What happens next is epic (Urban Dictionary, 2012). She leans into me without a word and kind of almost brushes her lips across my cheek. My mind is all high fives and smiley face icons. I would have stayed in that closet forever. But there is a pounding on the closet door. I turn the knob to open the door, trip over something that feels like a soccer ball, and then I realize what I'm falling over is my Abominable Snowman head.

I'll have to write the rest of the story in the next email because Mom is nagging me about having reached my limit on screen time today. Guess I'll go finish the next chapter of *Moby-Dick* for English or at least read the summary on Wikipedia real quick.

Later,

James the Abominable

From: the.darren.olmstead@gmail.com
To: whaleboy4ever@gmail.com
Date: December 15, 2012 at 3:56 PM
Subject: Dude!

Dude!

You're the hardest workin' man in *snow*-business!

I'm ecstatic for you about the kiss, brother! Beautiful creatures, those female types. And that one of 'em would even consider putting their lips on one of our kind—dudes,

I mean—truly boggles the mind sometimes. Your story makes me think about my whole Corinne thing a little differently. I feel lucky that I ever got to be with her, that we got to share what good times we did. We had tons of closet kisses, figuratively speaking (mostly), and they were absolutely thrilling, just like yours. Isn't that amazing? That another person can make you feel like your veins are flowing with liquid lightning? Much as I miss her, the mere fact that THOSE types of feelings are available even to someone like ME, is actually sort of amazing. (Note: this is a brand-spanking-new and likely temporary feeling, but for the moment, I'll take it over agonizing heartache, no questions asked.)

Also, this is nothing personal, just my observation as a person with a B.A. in Film Studies, but *one* cliffhanger in the party scene was cool. Two is making your audience a little impatient. You don't want to alienate your audience, dog.

So get on with it for Pete's sake (whoever Pete is—no one ever says)! Or at least for my sake! I have to hope that you didn't type your email with your only unbroken finger after Charlie Coxson beat the crap out of you.

Waiting in Vain,

Darren and the Wailers

From: whaleboy4ever@gmail.com
To: the.darren.olmstead@gmail.com
Date: December 16, 2012 at 3:48 PM
Subject: RE: Dude!

D-nominator:

So where did I leave off? Smith's party. Oh yeah. Coming out of the closet. Without my yeti costume on. That's right, from the neck up, I'm James Turner and from the neck down, I'm still Chewbacca's cousin. When my eyes adjust to the basement track lighting, the first person I see is Coxson. He's gape-mouthed as a guppy. And it takes a minute, but then I realize that I'm NOT the Snowdude and I'm NOT James, but some strange hybrid creature. The only noise comes from the iPod playing, some song that is really famous and I've heard a million times on the radio. Should remember her name, but it's the one where the chick sings about being on the edge of glory?

Charlie cracks his knuckles then shoves me. Once, twice, maybe three times. I completely lose track. Then there I am: tripping over my big feet, falling onto my butt, waiting for the horror of whatever is coming next. For some messed-up reason, I smile. Coxson goes, "What's so funny?" And because I'm nervous and it got a laugh before and I don't know what to do, I say: "Your teeth. They're the color of pee." Kids are laughing and I wish I could disappear. Coxson takes a sip of his drink and then throws the rest in my face. The jungle juice is everywhere. A couple of people think I'm bleeding. The yeti costume is ruined.

Sam goes, "WTF?"

I figure he's talking to me. I wipe my mouth with the back of my paw and try to think of how to explain. All that comes to mind: Salt, Salt, Salt.

Then Sam says, "You're such an asshole sometimes."

I am about to agree with him when Sam hands a napkin to Sophia and stares Coxson down. That's when I get it. He's not talking to me, he's talking to Coxson. Reprimanding Coxson, rather. In front of everyone. And even though I know he's trying to play hero for Sophia, I want to convince myself that maybe he is sticking up for me too.

To make a long story short, Smith asks me to leave and I

start to walk home in the rain. Freezing rain, actually. Because it's about 33 degrees. Some poor kid splashing in puddles sees me and I think he might have peed himself. About a mile in, I come across a Pace stop and wait there in the shelter until the bus comes. I take off my yeti head when I get on the bus because I'm getting stares. The bus driver says I reek of alcohol and I don't have any money for the fare. Just before he kicks me off, Mrs. D'Angelo just appears and pays for me. All the way back to the subdivision, I sit next to Mrs. D'Angelo, thinking about how I almost kissed her granddaughter. And waiting. Waiting for a speech of some sort, or for her to say something. Anything. Mrs. D'Angelo is NEVER silent. But she just picks at the beads on her rosary until our stop. Then she links arms with me and we walk under her umbrella down the street.

On her porch, Mrs. D'Angelo searches her carpet bag of a purse for the key, unlocks the door, then directs me to go inside. I've been to Mrs. D'Angelo's house before for tutoring, and we always sit in her kitchen (which is spotless since she does the majority of cooking on this ancient stove in the basement). I plop down at the kitchen table out of habit, and she makes me espresso. No frothy milk, no sugar. Just plain espresso. It tastes like tar and I almost gag drinking it. Then Mrs. D'Angelo pours me three more of those tiny glasses. And the whole time, she's talking to me like I'm in AP Italian or something. She sounds mad too, but she always sounds mad when she speaks in Italian, almost like I should know stuff that I don't know. She pauses a couple of times, and I know she's waiting for me to say something. But I can't understand anything she's saying. I don't know if it's the alcohol or what. All I do is nod, smile, and repeat "si" like some dumb Rosetta Stone tourist.

When I finish the last of the espresso, Mrs. D'Angelo

leads me to a bedroom upstairs and motions for me to get under the covers before leaving and closing the door. The blanket on the bed smells like garlic, dusty attics, and something spicy. Maybe incense. There's a picture of Mr. Lucca, Sophia's dad, on the nightstand with a little cross made out of dead palms tucked into the frame. I toss and turn because it feels like Mr. Lucca's watching me. And I wonder if he could see me from heaven or whatever while I was in a closet with his daughter. The comforter's garlic smell is also starting to make me feel sick. So I tiptoe down the hall to find the bathroom.

The hall is decorated with pictures of people (saints?) enduring various forms of torture: one woman is bleeding from the head, another carries her own eyeballs on a tray like they're mini-meatball appetizers, and then there's this guy who is covered in arrows—a human dartboard. By now, I feel like I'm going to puke any minute. The first door I open is the laundry room. There's a little shrine on the folding table with a picture of Mary, candles, and a plastic bottle that reads "Holy Water" on a piece of masking tape. The second door is the bathroom, thank God. When I enter, I mistake the empty feet of Mrs. D's pantyhose dangling over the side of the tub for a snake's skin. My stomach is in my throat. There's no way I'm making it to the toilet. And I end up yacking in the bidet. Eventually, when I clean up and make it back to the bedroom, I take off the yeti costume and sleep. Two hours later, when Mrs. D wakes me up and sends me home, I feel old like I've slept through three decades.

At home, the lights are all out, and my dad is snoozing in front of some PBS special about memory loss, thank God. I grab two of my mom's Aleve out of the powder room medicine cabinet. Dad stirs, and I pray that he doesn't wake up because I suck at lying more than I suck at being an Abominable

Snowman at parties. Upstairs in my room, I scour the Web for a yeti costume that looks like the one that I'd "borrowed" from work and ruined. First, do you know how expensive A.S. costumes are? They are like upwards of a hundred bucks. Second, even if I had that money (which I don't because I spent my work money on memberships to different conservation societies and a new KitchenAid mixer in neon green), the soonest a suit would arrive with express shipping (another thirty bucks) would be three days after my next shift at work.

Lying sucks. And since I lied enough for one weekend, I told Chin Piercing that I'd borrowed the costume without asking and ruined it. He said that my next few checks would have to go directly toward the cost of a new costume. Apparently, Star Arcade only uses the finest yeti fakery. The costume they purchased was $158.76.

No joke,

J-Juiced

From: ciaosoph@gmail.com
To: saraannblakely@gmail.com
Date: December 22, 2012 at 8:47 PM
Subject: Christmas Guest

Hey Sara,

Happy almost Christmas!

I think that you and the fam are probably at that caroling party tonight. You might hate it, but just know that being forced to wear a little elf hat and sing with a bunch of adults who are tone deaf but well-meaning is nothing compared to what I had to endure today. I'd take a bad case of hat head any day over dinner with Albert Stevens.

Apparently, this whole dinner thing was planned without my knowledge. Mom invited Albert over for an early Christmas celebration since she knew there was no way in hell that Nonna would invite him over for the Seven Fishes dinner on Christmas Eve (aka the World Series of Eating). Mom only revealed that Albert was coming after an extra pizza showed up at the house. I had the joy of receiving Albert as he arrived because Mom was still doing her makeup. Here's a little taste of how the night went:

Albert: "Sophia? I've heard all about you from your mom."

Me: "I'm sure you have." (You've been on like three dates with Mom. Guess that makes you an expert on my family?)

Albert: "Your mom tells me that you're a vegetarian and a budding social activist."

Me: "Actually, that's my little sister, Anna Maria. I'm the tap dancer."

Albert (pointing at a picture in the foyer from one of my recitals): "This must be you, here?"

Me: "Yep." (And just in case Albert thinks that this is some kind of audition for a vacant role . . .) "Me and Dad."

Albert: "I bet he was your biggest fan."

Me: "I'm going to go check on my mom. See if she's ready."

Albert: "You know, Sophia, I've watched Ginger Rogers dance a thousand times in old movies. I still don't know how she manages to keep all those moves straight."

Me: "It's called choreography."

As you can tell from the script above, this was a scene no one would want to watch, let alone live. The rest of the night featured Mom talking incessantly, smiling too hard, and trying to make connections between Albert and me or Anna Maria that really weren't there. ("Looks like we all like olives on our pizza.") Then Albert gave us all gifts. He got Mom her favorite slippers, the very slippers I'd bought her already for Christmas. And there was something else—a cat. Or kitten, I should say. Albert had the nerve to give all this to Mom with Dad staring down at him from the picture on the fireplace. Albert gave me a gift, too (which I guess is mandatory when you are trying to kiss up to the kids of someone you like)— that Coach purse I wanted so bad. He didn't put a penny inside for good luck like you're supposed to. Nonna would go ballistic. The last thing we need is more bad luck.

    Love,

    Soph

From: saraannblakely@gmail.com
To: ciaosoph@gmail.com
Date: December 22, 2012 at 9:35 PM
Subject: RE: Christmas Guest

Soph-

    @ home. Sick-flare w/fever. Missed caroling prty. :) Call?

    XO,

    Sara

From: ciaosoph@gmail.com
To: saraannblakely@gmail.com
Date: December 22, 2012 at 9:55 PM
Subject: RE: Christmas Guest

Hey Sara-

So sorry you got sick! How bad is your fever this time? Anyway, I can't call because I don't want Mom to hear me talking about Albert.

Love,

Soph

From: ciaosoph@gmail.com
To: saraannblakely@gmail.com
Date: December 23, 2012 at 9:14 PM
Subject: RE: Christmas Guest

Hey Sara-

So here's what I couldn't say earlier on the phone. The cat, Baby, is a complete disaster. Albert called tonight during dinner and Mom left the table—and her soup. The stupid cat started lapping up soup from Mom's bowl. Nonna hates cats so she's been carrying a spray bottle with vinegar in her apron pocket since Baby arrived. Once Baby jumped on the table to get the soup, Nonna aimed and spritzed wildly, one blast catching me in the face. The vinegar burned my eyes, smeared the room into a fog. I heard Italian curse words and Nonna's house slippers shuffling as she chased Baby through the kitchen. Then there was the sound of Anna Maria—who's got to be the youngest card-carrying member of PETA—begging Nonna to stop assaulting Baby. Of course, Mom was completely oblivious, still on the phone with Albert in the other room.

Anna Maria's pleas became louder, more urgent, and then . . . there was a crash. Once I rubbed enough of the vinegar out of my eyes, I saw Mom standing in front of me, slightly out of breath. Anna Maria was picking up pieces of a glass. Nonna had returned her spray bottle to her apron pocket holster. And there was Baby. The stupid cat cowered under the table until Mom convinced him to come to her.

Mom: "What happened?"

Me: "It's Baby. He's messing up everything, Mom."

Nonna: "In my house, animals, dey were not pets. We keep dem outside until we get hungry—"

Anna Maria: "God, that's so inhumane."

Nonna: "The mouse traps Peter put in the cellar, dey still work, no?"

Mom: "I got rid of those this summer. They were just collecting dust."

All I want for Christmas? For that cat to disappear.

Love,

Soph

From: saraannblakely@gmail.com
To: ciaosoph@gmail.com
Date: December 23, 2012 at 10:04 PM
Subject: RE: Christmas Guest

I'm allergic 2 cats. We'll have 2 hang @ my house frm now on.

Do u think Sam Pick wud go w/me 2 Turnabout? Who r u asking?

<3,

Sara

P.S. Can I borrow ur Coach bag?

From: ciaosoph@gmail.com
To: saraannblakely@gmail.com
Date: December 23, 2012 at 10:18 PM
Subject: RE: Christmas Guest

Hey Sara,

Purse: The thing is total trash. It's so small. I can't fit my life inside. At least the old one accommodated phone, wallet, Saint Jude prayer card, my lucky pig, lip gloss, keys, emergency tampon, etc. I didn't realize how well it held everything. Until now.

You and Sam: So cute.

Turnabout: Can't say. I want it to be a surprise!

Love,

Soph

From: the.darren.olmstead@gmail.com
To: whaleboy4ever@gmail.com
Date: December 27, 2012 at 1:31 PM
Subject: RE: Dude!

Bummer about the punched-up suit. At least the red all over you was spiked juice and not your own gushing blood. I realize I'm being a bit of a silver-lining searcher, but sometimes it's comforting to know that things could have been worse, like if Mrs. D hadn't been on that bus. Which is something to consider the next time you find yourself around some booze. Booze is tricky. As a person who has turned bad decision-making into a kind of high art, I can say with confidence that booze has factored heavily in some of my all-time worst choices. Anyway, I hope you've paid off your debt to Star Arcade society by now. And I hope the social waters have calmed since then and you're navigating them with ease.

Merry holidays and all that jazz,

D

From: MargaretAOlmstead@hotmail.com
To: Ktolmsteadmommy@gmail.com
Date: December 28, 2012 at 4:37 PM
Subject: Two Peas

Well, well. How are my wonderful grandbabies? Still perfect, I'm assuming. Christmas in south Florida is a bit of an odd proposition. We all went down to the beach this morning just because you can, even though it was cool and breezy and not quite an ideal beach day. I enjoyed the sun, but the company left something to be desired. Although it was enlightening.

I'm always looking for things that your brother and father have in common, and I don't often find too much. But I could see it today. We rode down to the beach. We parked. We walked out and lay down a towel. And in all this time, neither your Dad nor Darren said a single word. For some reason, the only time either of those two are quiet is around the other, but they're usually not this bad. So when Darren went and dove in the water for a few minutes, I asked your father what was wrong, and it turned out the whole reason he was sulky was because he'd run into McDowell High's football coach at the grocery store when he was going to pick up a Christmas ham. That was three days ago, and the state semifinal game Henson lost to McDowell was two months ago! He said, "I know, I'm pathetic." And I said to forget pathetic. It was downright unhealthy. Life is too short to be sad for two months about a high school football game. He said he hadn't been sad for two months, just that seeing the McDowell guy reminded him of how hard it was to lose the game. "But you've lost playoff games before. Why's this one different?" I asked, and he said it was because of how they'd lost. I asked him how, and your father, ever the model of elocution, said, "This kid, this kid I really like, this kid—not the best player, but a good kid, has some struggles but really a good kid—he totally screwed the pooch on the last play of the game. I mean big time. As in we probably woulda won if he hadn't messed up." He said the kid had been having problems and playing poorly leading up to that game and he probably should've been benched, but Dad had been giving him extra chances because he knew the kid had been having a hard time at home, and that just ended up causing them to lose and the other kids to be mad at the kid who botched the play.

By that time, Darren had come back. His swim consisted mostly of letting out primal screams and moans about how cold the water was, diving down below then popping back up and screaming in joyful agony again. I can remember him doing the exact same thing on vacation at the beach when he was about eight. Anyway, as we were walking to the car I asked him what was up, and he went into this big thing about how Corinne had left this residue on all of his senses—I don't have to tell you all of it, it's how he always talks—but he'd been making good headway in not hearing her voice in his head as often but that now it was back.

So there you have it. The Olmstead men: fall hard and heal slow. Beyond that, they can't agree on anything.

Love,

Mom

P.S. Hug and kiss those grandbabies for me!

JANUARY 2013

From: whaleboy4ever@gmail.com
To: the.darren.olmstead@gmail.com
Date: January 5, 2013 at 7:45 AM
Subject: RE: Dude!

Dear Darren,

Christmas consisted of me watching made-for-TV specials like "I Want a Dog for Christmas, Charlie Brown." Ever notice how none of the adults in Charlie Brown movies speak English? The teacher sounds like an off-tune trombone. It's pretty freaking weird. Anyway, Mom and Dad also got me a new tennis racket—something I'll never use. Given that the tennis instructor who gave me lessons for three years finally told Dad to save his money last spring, there are only two possible reasons that they got me this gift:

1) Dad played in college, and he still holds out hope that I might actually return one of his serves one day.

2) Tennis is a game you have to play with another person (which, of course, feeds Mom's whole social interaction crusade).

What I really wanted for Christmas was the complete collection of all *Whale Wars* seasons on DVD.

2013 has gotten off to a rough start. Ever since Smith's party, things at work have been pretty bad. Chin Piercing's got me on a tight leash, which means that I can't leave the break room to snag a slice of pizza from the snack station for lunch. Blunt, the guy who "cooks" in the snack station, won't give me anything for free anymore either. Not even nachos (and I'm pretty sure that the cheese is made from paper cement or at least a derivative of glue). Blunt stole a dollar a day from the cash register for a whole year, which is a lot worse than soiling an Abominable Snowman costume. But now, he acts like the Pope around me.

How was your holiday?

Sincerely,

James

From: the.darren.olmstead@gmail.com
To: whaleboy4ever@gmail.com
Date: January 11, 2013 at 6:31 PM
Subject: Holiday In

Hey there James,

Christmas was weird. My sis and her family weren't there, and my parents moved to West Palm Beach after I graduated because my dad got a job coaching there. He says Florida's a "hotbed for football." It's definitely hot. I like 75 degree weather as much as the next guy, but it's a little creepy on Christmas.

My dad got all his questions out of the way the first night about what I was going to do with myself since I'm not working at Testy Snobbin. While I was getting grilled, my mom jumped in with a question about what my dad was doing at twenty-three, and after much hemming, hawing, and listing of mitigating factors—mainly that he'd lived at home and had a part-time job while he was in college, and hence his schooling had cost his folks closer to 8 Gs than 80—he acknowledged that on his first Christmas after college graduation he'd just gotten home from a "summer" of backpacking in Europe that had lasted until December. This exchange followed:

"But I was working the last two months I was there," he said.

"Doing what?" she said.

"Being an English-language tour guide in Rome."

"And you just quit?" I said.

"I didn't major in tour guiding!"

"You didn't major in football coaching either," I said.

"Blah blah blargh blargety bleat spriggety 80 thousand dollars!" (Approximate translation.)

This was mellower than he used to be, though. When I was in high school and college, he basically parented me like a football coach: lots of yelling when he was mad, lots of motivational speeches (it was halftime probably twice a week at our house), and high fives when I aced a test. I'm surprised he didn't throw in a butt-smack every now and again, but luckily I never wore football pants.

After that first night, though, we had a good time. There was, of course, football to watch, and I like watching it with my dad. He's in his element. After a lot of plays he leans back, puts his hands behind his head, and says, "You see what happened there?" I usually respond by saying something cheeky like, "Yes. The man threw a ball to the other man while some other men crashed into each other." He just ignores me and goes into this really detailed explanation of the play and why it worked or failed. It's like listening to my favorite film professor from school talk about a scene. He's so deep inside it all. But that's nothing compared to when he's actually coaching. When his players perfectly execute a play that he designed, I think that's about the happiest he can be. I hope one day to have a job that excites me that much and that I can get that deep inside of. The closest I think I've ever gotten was when I was editing my senior film project. It was a six-minute short my buddy wrote about a guy hanging out at his apartment by himself. It was exactly as boring as it sounds, but when I was trying to edit it, I'd be sifting through the takes, trying to arrange them into a story that actually made sense and said something about this guy's life, and I'd look up and see that three hours had passed in what felt like twenty minutes.

On this trip home, though, all I've been able to focus on was the one thing I need to not be focusing on: Corinne. I was doing good. I really was. But I'm pretty bored because I don't have any friends here. So I was sitting around, and because I'm an idiot, I was streaming KCRW, my favorite indie radio station from back in LA, and wouldn't you know it, they play an interview with the Tipsy Gypsies. "Who?" you ask. Corinne's band, that's who! Argh! Anyway, she was charming as usual. Here's a part of the transcript that I may or may not have made myself.

KCRW: So, Corinne. I can't help but notice, there's something, I don't know, different about you compared to the rest of the band.
Corinne: You're correct. Not many people notice right off that I'm the kind of person who wins in poker and all the rest of these poor things are the kind who don't.
Steven Jetton: We just feel sorry for you on account of you having to haul that bass around all the time.

Corinne: Well, I appreciate the sympathy. But I never take it easy on him, even when the Civil War flashbacks are messing with his sleep.

(howling laughter from the band)

KPST: I didn't know the age difference was that extreme, but at 22, you are considerably younger than the rest of the band. How did you meet these guys?

Corinne: Well, I'd been a fan of Steve and Emily and Bobby's playing since I was a little girl. I grew up in Oakland, but my parents were teachers and loved to travel around to bluegrass festivals all summer. So I saw all these guys play a hundred times before I ever played with them. Eventually I started bringing my bass with me on the trips. We all jammed together at a festival up outside of San Luis Obispo when I was eighteen, and they haven't been able to get rid of me since.

I know I've talked a lot about Corinne but haven't mentioned many of the particulars of the breakup. And that's mostly because I still hadn't been quite able to make sense of it myself. But hearing that interview drudged up a lot of memories, and now some of it's becoming clear. I've been sifting through the footage, trying to make sense of it. Reading that interview, I realized that I was so jealous of all the attention she got because she's such a rare creature—a beautiful, sharp-tongued, bass-playing semi-hippie in the land of plastic surgery and gourmet restaurants for dogs—that I got totally paranoid and tried to go to every gig she had because I was sure that if I didn't, she'd meet her male equivalent, some banjo player with six-pack abs and a Harvard degree to fall back on, and leave me in a second. I basically did the Gollum from *Lord of the Rings* "My precious!" thing, only with a person instead of a ring. Eventually, the (in hindsight) utterly predictable process played out: paranoia, smothering, getting dumped.

In a moment of weakness the other night, I logged onto the Book of Faces and memorized every pixel of every picture of her and her new boyfriend and had the following realization: Crap, he's not even new anymore. Been almost a year.

All right, back to the Internetwork to search for gainful employment (and not look at the Book of Faces. So. Hard. Not to. Though.).

DarrenSearchOfJob

From: whaleboy4ever@gmail.com
To: the.darren.olmstead@gmail.com
Date: January 17, 2013 at 11:21 PM
Subject: RE: Holiday In

Dear D-bomb:

I've been thinking about your email and the Facebook stuff with Corinne. Why hasn't she unfriended you? Maybe that's a good sign?

Sincerely,

Jam-in'

From: the.darren.olmstead@gmail.com
To: whaleboy4ever@gmail.com
Date: January 25, 2013 at 7:21 PM
Subject: Workin' it

Eh. I doubt it. I'm pretty sure she's either just being polite or she actually wouldn't mind being my friend. I'm not sure which is worse. I imagine that the Friend Zone with Corinne would be pretty unbearable since I used to occupy the

More-Than-a-Friend Zone. If I were some sort of emotional Superman, I could maybe stand it, but alas, I'm not.

But I have some good news to report. I got a J-O-B! I was really close to becoming an insurance man with Luke, but then I stumbled across an ad for an after-school program job at this middle school in town. I started thinking about the time I spent volunteering at your school, and then I started thinking about how cool it's been getting to know you recently, so I applied. I got the job, and I have you to thank. So thanks!

I work with sixth and seventh graders, much less mature than old men such as yourself. It's hard to believe a fart could have brought me such a mixture of glee, pride, hilarity, embarrassment, and general big-deal-ness as it does the boys here, but I suppose it did. The girls ain't perfect either, but their ridiculousness tends to come out in slightly less ridiculous ways, if that makes any sense. You'd like the teacher I work with. She doesn't take any crap, that's for sure. I can be doing everything I can to get them to be quiet and it's like I'm not even in the room, and she can say two words and give them this crazy death-scowl and they hush up in a millisecond. Impressive. I've gotta work on that death scowl. Anyway, it's good to have a little income coming in, and I don't have to get coffee for people or get sore shoulders holding a boom mic over my head for hours.

It's a tiring gig, though, for sure. I'm WIPED when I get home. But I'm still carving out time to watch docs and cast about for what would be a great subject for one. I have a notebook full of ideas, but none of them are quite singing to me yet.

Keep it breezy,

Darren aka Mr. Olmstead

From: whaleboy4ever@gmail.com
To: the.darren.olmstead@gmail.com
Date: January 27, 2013 at 3:40 PM
Subject: RE: Workin' It

Dear Mr. Olmstead,

Things have been nuts here. I heard that someone (read: Coxson) started a Facebook page in my name ("Whale Boy") as a joke—complete with a picture of me at Smith's in the yeti costume and a doctored version of my school photo where I have a blowhole on the top of my head and baleen teeth. I can't confirm any of this as I am not on Facebook because I've never cared to waste time reading about who is "in a relationship" or what music people "like." I'm pretty sure that the Facebook page with my name was started as a joke and the goal was to make sure that I had ZERO friends.

I guess that kind of backfired because my page has gone viral (at least according to this kid in my Advanced Calc class) and now I have something like 1,000 "friends." At school, it's like I'm a celebrity—fist bumps, high fives, even the occasional butt smack. Any other kid would be in his glory. But I wish I could just float through the hall like plankton. Like before.

Sincerely,
Average James

From: sduckett@gnewc.org
To: pbrammer@gnewc.org
Date: February 1, 2013 at 8:20 AM
Subject: Wax Floors

Hi Peter,

Is it ok if I wax the floors in your office since you're out of town? How's FL?

—Stanley P. Duckett

From: pbrammer@gnewc.org
To: sduckett@gnewc.org
Date: February 1, 2013 at 8:21 AM
Subject: Out of the Office

Thank you for your email. I am currently out of the office until 2/6/13 and I will have infrequent access to email. For immediate help, please contact Steven Kauffman at skauffman@gnewc.org. I look forward to speaking with you upon my return.

Best,

Peter

From: pbrammer@gnewc.org
To: sduckett@gnewc.org
Date: February 1, 2013 at 9:31 AM
Subject: RE: Wax Floors

Dear Stanley,

You might want to hold off on waxing the floors. I might be back sooner than I thought. I was supposed to meet my sister last night at a local crab shack for dinner. In my backpack, I had a gift-wrapped vegan cookbook and a bracelet inscribed with: "God grant me the serenity to accept the things I cannot change." The bracelet was silver—which always looked so good against Elsie's pale skin—and the woman in the store told me that the inscription was part of a serenity prayer, something that former addicts say in recovery. I also took the shells Elsie sent me in a little box. My plan was to give them back to her so that she could use any money from selling them to take a college class.

So I waited at the crab shack. Had one beer. Two. Three. After two hours, Elsie still hadn't showed. I walked over to the harbor where she told me she keeps her boat/house docked and asked around. This guy cleaning a fishing boat knew her. Called her Angel. He said she and her boyfriend made regular drug runs down to Mexico, and that they never came back from the last one in January. There was a Coast Guard search, but it didn't turn up anything. He said that no one knew she had kin or else they would have gotten in touch. I tried to tell him that his story couldn't be true. That I'd talked to her on New Year's Day and she said she was enrolling in a community college to take classes. I told him that she collected shells and helped her boyfriend fish for a living. That she'd been sober for eleven months. That she was a vegan yogi, for Christ's sake. He shook his head sadly and turned back on his hose. The water gushed so loudly onto the boat's deck that I could barely hear him. "She's a sleepwalker," I think he said, injecting an invisible syringe into his arm.

Best,

Peter

From: jolmstead@hensonacademyfl.org
To: the.darren.olmstead@gmail.com
Date: February 3, 2013 at 7:00 AM
Subject: New Job

Darren,

Congratulations on the new job, son. I don't have any advice that you're not already sick of hearing, so I won't bother. I know you can be successful at whatever you put your mind to.

Dad

From: the.darren.olmstead@gmail.com
To: jolmstead@hensonacademyfl.org
Date: February 4, 2013 at 7:21 PM
Subject: RE: New Job

Aw, Dad!

Dang, that was like the sweetest thing I ever did hear!

Thanks! I will make sure not to waste this opportunity.

Big things in the offing! Would tell you but don't want to jinx anything.

Darren

From: the.darren.olmstead@gmail.com
To: realhardbard@gmail.com
Date: February 5, 2013 at 4:27 PM
Subject: Room on the Couch?

Hey there Sash,

What's the good word—or shall I say verse? Much as I love the left coast, I'm considering a trip back east the first week of March. Got an idea for a film project. My folks moved to Florida a few months back, so I was wondering if I could crash with you since I'm gonna be shooting in Philly.

You still carting around aristocrats in those rolling black behemoths, or is poetry paying the bills now?

Gimme a call. I broke my phone a while back and lost all my contacts.

Talk soon,

Darren

From: pbrammer@gnewc.org
To: elsietheexcellent@yahoo.com
Date: February 5, 2014 at 5:31 PM
Subject: PLEASE CALL

Dear Elsie-

I know that you probably don't check this email any more. But I am desperate. I flew to Florida, went to Bub's

Crab Shack like we planned, waited three hours. When you didn't show up, I walked over to the dock where you said you keep your boat. Some guy there told me that you and your boyfriend went on a trip to Mexico and that you didn't return. I don't care what your circumstances might be. And I'm not mad. I just want to find you.

 Love,
 Peter

From: mailer-daemon@yahoo.com
To: pbrammer@gnewc.org
Date: February 5, 2014 at 5:32 PM
Subject: Returned mail-nameserver error report

Message not delivered to the following:

 elsietheexcellent No matches to nameserver query

 ————Error Detail (phquery V4.4 (yahoo), $Revision: 1.62 $):

 The message, "No matches to nameserver query," is generated whenever the ph nameserver fails to locate either a ph alias or name field that matches the supplied name. The usual causes are typographical errors or the use of nicknames. Recommended action is to use the ph program to determine the correct ph alias for the individuals addressed. If ph is not available, try sending to the most explicit form of the name, e.g., if mike-fox fails, try michael-fox or michael-j-fox.

From: jolmstead@hensonacademyfl.org
To: kerickson@hensonacademyfl.org
Date: February 6, 2013 at 7:00 AM
Subject: Dark Days

That's how I refer to these months between the Super Bowl and the beginning of two-a-days come August. It's a little bit exaggerational I know, but I just get so antsy. Happens every year. But this year it's starting off worse because it was my first year and there are so many things I want to adjust going into next season. To come up just short like we did. I've not had a peaceful night of sleep since that McDowell game. Then you look back at all those practices and all those hours designing plays and watching video and redesigning plays, and you think, "If I'd have just done one little thing different, we might be Florida Class 2A champions right now." Maybe insert a nickel package on third down. Find a variation on our fake punt play. (Can you imagine if we'd pulled off a fake punt against McDowell with 4:34 left in the fourth quarter and then scored with under a minute left? I get goose bumps just thinking about it.)

So, my wife is bugging me to play golf with her next weekend, which, okay, sure, I'll do that. It's one of the advantages of living down here. But she wants to play 18 holes, and I just don't know if I can handle waiting around for her to take four strokes to get to the green. But just as I don't lie to my players, I will not lie to my wife, so that's why I'm writing to see if we could set up an off-season coaches' meeting this Saturday afternoon so that I can truthfully tell her that I only have time to play nine holes. Let me know.

Jack

From: the.darren.olmstead@gmail.com
To: whaleboy4ever@gmail.com
Date: February 6, 2013 at 11:31 PM
Subject: Doc-tor

Jimmy Rotator,

'Tis quite an interesting situation you've got there. You find yourself alienated at work as a result of your stained uniform, yet a kind of folk hero at school because of your whale work. Your enemies' attempts to vanquish you have only made you stronger, as if you were a fire that they tried to douse with gasoline. And now, now they've turned you into a raging inferno! Well, more of a brooding, insecure inferno, which might well be more interesting than the traditional smoke-'n'-flame job. This fire's got some substance beyond carbon dioxide, water vapor, oxygen, and nitrogen (I swear I didn't just do a search for what fire's made of. Really. Hold on, need to clear my browsing history before anyone checks). The question is, will this crazy amount of oxygen (i.e. high fives, butt smacks, and other forms of attention) sustain the conflagration that is you, or will the attention turn out to be a flame retardant and end up snuffing out our poor hero? Honestly, I don't know the answers.

But I will. Everyone IN THE WORLD will.

What am I talking about? Well, nice of you to mentally ask. Check it: since I'm back on a school schedule, I have a spring break. Spring break!!! Should I go to Cancun? South Padre? Jamaica? See if I can win a wet T-shirt contest? See if I can get a date with the winner of a wet T-shirt contest? See if I can get kicked out of a wet T-shirt contest?

NO! That's all CollegeDarren stuff. (Real Talk: One of those wet T-shirt scenarios actually happened during spring break my junior year, but you'll just have to guess which one.)

CollegeDarren is gone, replaced by the new-and-improved Post-CollegeDarren (conjure an image of me standing with hands on hips, clad in tights and cape, a PCD emblem on my chest). PCD is done obsessing over his disastrous breakup and is now treating his brief stint as a production assistant on a crappy TV show as a learning experience rather than a defeat. Thus, PCD isn't going to waste his spring break being wasted, he's going to pursue his passion: documentary filmmaking!

My subject? Well, interesting that again you should mentally ask.

I want to make a film about something interesting but off the beaten path, a subject that could really draw people in, that is unique, and that I find personally fascinating, that means something to me. Something I connect with.

Well, I finally found the subject that sings to me. And he's singing whale songs.

What better subject could I find than a young man with an uncanny knowledge and deep passion for humpback whales who has at the same time managed to compensate for certain social eccentricities by wearing an Abominable Snowman costume when hanging out with his friends?

It's perfect! What do you say? I bring my Canon up there, get some footage of you doing your thing, tape some interviews, and begin editing as soon as I get back. If necessary, I go back to Philly this summer to see how things are going and do some pick-up shots. I'm so psyched about this project, James. I'm checking sale fares right now. Let me know what you think!

Later,

DarrInspired

From: kerickson@hensonacademyfl.org
To: jolmstead@hensonacademyfl.org
Date: February 7, 2013 at 5:45 PM
Subject: RE: Dark Days

You kidding me, Jack? You have a wife who will play golf with
you and you're complaining? You outside your mind, man.
Football season don't start for six damn months! Hit the links
with your lady. And try not to be designing plays in your mind
while you do it. Get the McDowell game out of your mind.
It'll be good for you.
    Keith

From: whaleboy4ever@gmail.com
To: the.darren.olmstead@gmail.com
Date: Febraury 23, 2013 at 3:22 PM
Subject: RE: Doc-tor

Dear Darren:
    Wow, you sound really excited. Which is good. The
breakups (with Corinne and then with Testy Snobbin) really
seemed to be eating away at you. I put off writing you back
for so long because I wasn't sure how to tell you. And now,
I'm pretty sure that it's too late. I want to help you with the
project, I do, Darren. I just don't know if I can do it. The
movie, that is. Like I said, I'm just not an interesting person.
    Later,
    James

From: the.darren.olmstead@gmail.com
To: whaleboy4ever@gmail.com
Date: February 23, 2013 at 9:07 PM
Subject: RE: Doc-tor

Hey there Jimmy Turn,

Oh, the many ways you are wrong about this one,
sir. You're probably curious about how you're wrong.
Conveniently, I'm going to tell you.

You said you couldn't do the movie. But the truth is,
you're ALREADY doing the movie. You're a living story,
man! You just don't know it. This wave is cresting at the
perfect time. I already bought my ticket to Philly, and I'll
be there Monday morning. We'll shoot a lot of interview
footage to get all this back-story down, get a couple shots of
you walking around in the Snow Dude suit, looking off into
the distance all pensively and stuff to set up what a complex
character you are, then I'll just trail you with the camera and
see what happens.

You also had the gall to say that you're not interesting.
Wrong again. Saying that you're not interesting is almost
comical in its wrongness, its wrong-ativity, its wrong-
naciousness. Wrong, wrong, wrong-a-long-a-ding-dong. The
human brain craves novelty, originality. You're a repository of
facts about humpback whales, and you obsess over the health
of certain whales as if they were blood relatives. Pardon me
for using all caps for this, but THIS IS NOT NORMAL,
JAMES! And that's a good thing. Who would want to go see
a documentary about some average-Joe ninth grader? I can
hear the voice-over for the trailer: "In a world of pizza and
pop music and porn GIFs on Tumblr . . . there is one kid
who . . . likes pizza and pop music and porn GIFs on Tumblr,
pretty much like all the other kids . . . In IMAX 3D this

summer (www.avgjoethefakemovie.com)." Bo-*ring*.

Now, as far as what you should do about being the face of whale advocacy at your school, I feel I shouldn't offer too much advice at this point, in order to maintain objectivity in my role as director, but I think the choice you've got to make is whether to embrace this newfound celebrity or discourage it. Embracing it could mean access to new friends, more opportunities to play Seven Minutes in Heaven, more appearances in the yearbook. But what would it do to your relationship with Sam and Sophia? (BTW, what's going on with Sophia? Can you tell if she digs the "Whale Boy" meme? It's something to consider, just sayin'.) Could being Whale Boy help bring attention to your cause, somehow help save other Salts before they perish? And rejecting the Whale Boy thing as your public identity carries its own risks. I mean, you really do love whales, so are you compromising your integrity by trying to be an "Average James ," as you put it?

Though I don't envy your dilemma, this is all great news from a filmmaking standpoint. I'm really excited for where this is headed, where things in general are headed for me. I'm employed; I'm pursuing my filmmaking dreams. I hate to admit it, but I don't know if I believed until recently that I was capable of all this. I hate even more to admit that I wish Corinne could see me now, see how I am now, you know? That she could see what she's missing, what she didn't know was there. (Several fast head shakes to snap out of it . . . and, I'm back.) Anyway, see you soon.

Best,

Darren

From: realhardbard@gmail.com
To: the.darren.olmstead@gmail.com
Date: February 26, 2013 at 4:27 PM
Subject: RE: Room on the Couch?

BODO!

Good to hear from you. Sorry I'm just now responding. I don't check this email much anymore. A kind editor at a literary magazine let me know that having it at the top of poems I submitted was probably working against me. Let me take a moment to remind you that getting this email address was your idea. Now I just keep it to sign up for free stuff that requires a valid email address. It's part of my effort to empty my mind so the poetry can flow in. By the way, I'm glad to see that you've moved on from ladiesandgentlementheamazingdarren@hotmail.com.

Yes, I'm still driving for Watson. Thanks for asking.

No, I'm not making any money from poetry, and no thanks for asking.

Sure, you can stay with me for a few days. Seeing you might be good for my poetry. Your presence will no doubt bring back memories of even more stupid things you convinced me to do with you during our high school tenure. Maybe I can translate the residual embarrassment into ideas for new poems.

Humbly,

Sash

From: the.darren.olmstead@gmail.com
To: whaleboy4ever@gmail.com
Date: February 28, 2013 at 2:07 AM
Subject: RE: Doc-tor

Jamesizzle,

Just say yes. We'll give ten percent of the proceeds from the film to an antipoaching organization.

Later,

Darren-ticing Offer

MARCH 2013

From: TrypTycker.com
To: the.darren.olmstead@gmail.com
Date: March 9, 2013 at 2:41 AM
Subject: Your Upcoming Trip

GAMMA Airlines confirmation code: HUFKM8 -
Your flight is confirmed.
　　TrypTyck Itinerary: 7661412731

　　Dear DARREN,
　　Almost time for your trip! We just wanted to remind you
about your Philadelphia flight reservation. We've saved this
information in your account. You do not need to reconfirm
with the airline(s) or TrypTycker. Happy travels!

From: the.darren.olmstead@gmail.com
To: whaleboy4ever@gmail.com
Date: March 11, 2013 at 6:30 AM
Subject: RE: Doc-tor

Uh, Jimmer? You there?
　　My flight leaves in like six hours. We cool?
　　Darr-uncertain

From: sduckett@gnewc.org
To: pbrammer@gnewc.org
Date: March 11, 2013 at 10:20 AM
Subject: Follow Up

Dear Peter—

Jan told me you were looking for me like an hour ago. You caught me. I was at DD grabbing a long john. I swung by your office but the lights were off. You out in the field for the rest of the day?

—Stanley Duckett

From: pbrammer@gnewc.org
To: sduckett@gnewc.org
Date: March 11, 2013 at 10:40 AM
Subject: RE: Follow Up

Dear Stanley:

Actually, I am working from home. I got a call from the officer who I filed my sister's missing person report with down in Florida. He had an update for me on Elsie's case and I felt that it would be better to take his call here. I just wanted to let someone know.

For my entire adult life, anything to do with Elsie has always stirred up a powerful cocktail of feelings—mostly hope but always with strong shots of disappointment. This time, I tried not to be too optimistic as I dialed the officer's number. Long story short, he told me that an emergency room in Miami received an overdose. The woman had no identification on her, but I guess she resembled my sister. Anyway, they're sending officers out to investigate and then they'll be in touch this afternoon. I was so shocked that I didn't think to ask whether the woman was alive or dead.

Best,

Peter

From: sduckett@gnewc.org
To: pbrammer@gnewc.org
Date: March 11, 2013 at 1:03 PM
Subject: RE: Follow Up

Peter,

I hope you get some good news. Sometimes, waiting's the hardest part. My twin brother was in a coma for 2 months a while back. I swear the coma was worse than his death.

—Stanley Duckett

From: pbrammer@gnewc.org
To: sduckett@gnewc.org
Date: March 11, 2013 at 3:55 PM
Subject: RE: Follow Up

Stanley—

It wasn't her.

Best,

Peter

From: whaleboy4ever@gmail.com
To: the.darren.olmstead@gmail.com
Date: March 12, 2013 at 3:05 PM
Subject: RE: Doc-tor

Hi D-Danger:

You okay? I hope you don't need me to come bail you out of jail or something.

Anyway, three thoughts popped into my head when you tapped my shoulder outside the Carlsburg cafeteria today:

1) I can't believe you actually came to Philadelphia.

2) You must have had to pay an extra airlines fee for all of that movie equipment you were lugging.

3) I forgot that you're kind of a short guy (maybe I had a growth spurt or something?).

I think I probably should have said #1 to you as a greeting. Sorry that I actually said #3. Good thing the camera wasn't rolling yet.

Just so you know, I don't usually eat lunch in the hall outside of the cafeteria at a table by myself. Typically, I sit at the end of the table with a bunch of kids in my Bio and Advanced Calc classes and we all do our homework. But I'd been doing a lot of thinking since your last email and, with some trepidation, I decided that maybe you were right. Until your email, it never occurred to me that my newfound celebrity as Whale Boy might be an opportunity to spread the word about Salt's brethren and their plight. I got pretty excited about the idea of trying to educate people about humpback whale endangerment. And so, using the moniker Salt, I joined FB and started to post information on the Whale Boy page. Mostly information about humpbacks, a whale song or two, and some pics—head shots and a couple of really nice fluke close-ups too.

People started to "like" my posts and left all sorts of comments. Some favorite examples:

1) "That whale should try out 4 CHS Glee"

2) "Booked it—Spring Break 2013 Boston. Fenway, College Tours, and Whale Watching"

I also shared this awesome article about new research on how humpback whales have passed down lobtail feeding techniques to one another through cultural transmission and the social relationships. Basically, when the herring population took a nose dive back in the '80s, a few whales figured they could slap their tails on the water to hunt new kinds of fish, and today 40 percent of the population is using that hunting strategy.

There is a great quote in the article from one of the study's authors, Dr. Hoppitt: "We can learn more about the forces that drive the evolution of culture by looking outside our own ancestral lineage and studying the occurrence of similar attributes in groups that have evolved in a radically different environment to ours, like the cetaceans" (Allen, J., Weinrich, M., Hoppitt, W. & Rendell L., *ScienceDaily*, 2013).

Sam shared that quote on his FB page and wrote "Dig it," which made me smile. Sophia responded with <3, which I think means heart or love (Google, 2013). What she loves is open to interpretation, but Sam told me in Bio that the rumor is she is going to ask him to Turnabout, this high school dance where the girls ask the guys.

Anyway, when you found me outside of the cafeteria, it was because I decided to start a campaign to raise funds for Carlsburg High School to adopt a whale. You couldn't really see yesterday because the period was over and the bell had already rung, but usually there is a line of people waiting to put money into my cashbox. In fact, in less than a week, I think we've actually generated enough funds to adopt an entire pod! Maybe you can get that on camera tomorrow if they let you back in.

    See you soon (I hope),

    J-ammin'

From: Paul Tedoni
To: FacultyStaffGroup
Date: March 12, 2013 at 4:45 PM
Subject: Trespassing Incident

Hello Everyone,

    As most of you are aware by now, there was an incident involving a young man trying to shoot unauthorized video inside the school. He actually came to me asking for permission first, but due to liability and distraction concerns, I told him he was not allowed to. He politely thanked me for my time and said he would be on his way, but he must have gone down the hall away from the main doors instead of toward them.

    Despite the intruder's rather youngish looks, Mr. Dobson quickly identified him as a non-student and escorted him from the premises. I witnessed the end of this altercation from the teacher's lounge window as I was bending down to retrieve a diet root beer from the vending machine, and from where I stood, it appeared the young man was quite terrified of Mr. Dobson. Considering that he appeared to be nearly nauseated with fear, I doubt he will make any similar attempts in the future, but just to be safe, be on the lookout. The trespasser appeared to be about eighteen to twenty years old, of average build, about five and a half feet tall, with short brown hair and sporting a rather feeble attempt at a beard.

    Keep up the good work. Spring break is almost here.

    Paul Tedoni, MEd

    Principal, Carlsburg High School

From: whaleboy4ever@gmail.com
To: pbrammer@gnewc.org
Date: March 12, 2013 at 5:00 PM
Subject: Donation?

Dear Peter Brammer, PhD,

    I had your email from an inquiry about a whale earlier last year. My current concern is regarding a sizable donation I sent exactly one week ago via post mail to GNEWC. Would you please confirm receipt of a check at your earliest convenience? I have additional funds to send, but I need some reassurance first that the first installment arrived safely.

    Sincerely,

    James Turner

From: pbrammer@gnewc.org
To: whaleboy4ever@gmail.com
Date: March 12, 2013 at 5:17 PM
Subject: RE: Donation?

Dear Mr. Turner:

    On behalf of the Greater New England Whale Conservancy, I would like to personally thank you for your generous donation. I apologize as you should have received correspondence from the Development Department (not sure what happened there). Given your interest in humpbacks, I wanted to share more information with you regarding the work that your donations support. My team and I are currently researching the possible causes of death of several juveniles that beached in the last year to determine whether human interference or disease played a role. I will keep you updated as I understand you care deeply about this species and its plight and I apologize for any past lapses in communication on my part. Again, we appreciate your generosity.

Best,

Peter Brammer, PhD

From: the.darren.olmstead@gmail.com
To: whaleboy4ever@gmail.com
Date: March 12, 2013 at 11:09 PM
Subject: Hola

Evening, Jamestown,

I've been perusing the Whale Boy FB page, and there's some really interesting stuff here. Congrats on raising awhaleness—ahem, awareness (sorry, I had to; I'm a hopeless pun-maker).

I don't know if you've seen this yet, but someone named Edgar Allen Poacher left a really bizarre comment :

Hey Salt, got summer vacay plans? I heard Saint Vincent and the Grenadines is nice that time of year. LOL.

Then:

Hope you get asked to Turn About. Our GROUP is gonna be ROWDY! (Mennissing laugh)

You'd think someone who named himself on FB after a poet would know how to spell "menacing."

Last, there's a very cryptic one from someone by the name Herman Whaleville. It says, "He who has never failed somewhere, that man can not be great." It's a real quote by Herman Melville, the *Moby-Dick* guy.

Any idea what any of that stuff means?

No worries about earlier. It wasn't your fault that my booty got booted today. I knew about the security restrictions and the waivers to appear on camera. In fact, I discussed them at length with Mr. Tedoni earlier that morning. He didn't seem to understand my artistic vision one iota, and for that I can't really blame him. He's a high school principal: being boring and careful and tight-sphinctered is in both his DNA and his job description. But those qualities are not in my genes. I couldn't be a filmmaker if they were.

It's no problem, though, because I have a plan: Tomorrow I show up for the 10 a.m. school tour, work myself in the group for a while, then catch you at lunch, cell phone video camera only. We'll get that cool shaky-camera vibe they used in the first *Hunger Games* movie. It'll be sweet.

Just have to make sure and avoid that Dobson fellow. Not a big dude, but he's got a grip like a vice. I can't repeat what he said about me here, but he was up in my face and I can say with certainty that he'd eaten a tuna sandwich sometime in the last couple of hours, and I was well on the way to being able to discern whether he'd had yellow or spicy brown mustard on it by the time he finally ended his diatribe and shoved me out the side door of the building.

Regardless of what happens at lunch, let's catch up after school. Can you chat during your break at Star Arcade? I talked to your boss, and he was into the whole promotional angle, so I'm okay to film there.

See you tomorrow, dog,

Dare-ya

From: saraannblakely@gmail.com
To: ciaosoph@gmail.com
Date: March 12, 2013 at 11:10 PM
Subject: Turnabout

Sam got letter I sent asking him 2 Turnabout. He txted me &
said he'll let me know soon. (WTF?) Can u tell me who u r
asking? I think he wants 2 go w/u.
    TTFN,
    Sara
    P.S. No skool 2morrow. Tests @ Children's.

From: whaleboy4ever@gmail.com
To: the.darren.olmstead@gmail.com
Date: March 12, 2013 at 11:15 PM
Subject: RE: Hola

Dear D-ang:
    Well, we didn't get to talk about it today at lunch, but I
think we're both pretty sure of Edgar Allan Poacher's identity.
Those comments that he left on Facebook? There's an island
in the Grenadines that's like the only place the International
Whaling Commission allows humpbacks to be hunted. The
natives there are allowed to hunt up to four times a year. It's
some cultural thing, I think. Oh, and the "rowdy" group
comment from Poacher? When male whales are courting a
female, they're called "rowdy" as they slap each other with
their fins, snap their jaws, do peduncle throws, lunge, breach,
and hold themselves under water. In other words, this Poacher
is smart.
    I'm guessing that you got the whole episode today on
video with your phone. (How did the shaky video effect work

out? I felt kind of seasick after watching *Hunger Games*, but it might've just been indigestion from eating two boxes of Sour Patch Kids). Did you manage to nab any footage before Dobson grabbed you by the neck? I appreciate you trying to stick up for me and I'm sorry that it meant you inhaled vast quantities of Dobson's breath as he escorted you down the music wing to the exit for the SECOND time this week. (Onion rings were the special at our cafeteria today. Better than tuna though, right?) Anyway, I'm curious about where you got your moves. You were a regular Jackie Chan today. I think I saw Coxson wipe at his cheek after. Not sure if it was blood or tears.

Make no mistake, I, too, was cheesed off today at lunch (Urban Dictionary, 2013). Not just for myself, but for Sophia too. Such a dumb prank. To block out the laughing and all the auxiliary meanness associated with Coxson's joke, I just kept thinking about this article I read recently about how sperm whale feces (called "ambergris")—this seemingly worthless and, well, unattractive thing—can fetch thousands of dollars on the market and is used to make expensive perfumes like Chanel No. 5.

But not even strange and wonderful ambergris could distract me from the poster taped to my Adopt-a-Whale table: "For one night, be my Moby-Dick—at Turnabout, it is you I pick. —Sophia." Of course, I knew the prank was undoubtedly the work of the Poacher (aka Coxson). The point of Turnabout is for girls to ask guys in very strange ways. Kimberly Trout asked Steven Mark by writing "take me to Turnabout" in ketchup on a cafeteria table. But any idiot would know that the poster was written by Coxson or one of his goons thanks to the stupid "slap my tail" comment in totally different handwriting below the invite.

Still, I couldn't help hoping. And I couldn't take my

eyes off of it. Reminds me of the time I saw a nude girl on a magazine cover in a bookstore with my mom. You can't look away no matter how embarrassed it makes you feel.

In solidarity,

J-ville

From: ciaosoph@gmail.com
To: saraannblakely@gmail.com
Date: March 13, 2013 at 2:31 PM
Subject: RE: Turnabout

Dear Sara,

In study hall. Just got your email. Had dance practice after school. I hope the tests went well, but I'm not going to lie, I could have used your support at school today. I finally got around to asking my date to Turnabout, and let's just say that it didn't go as planned. At. All.

I didn't tell you (or Becky) who I was going to ask because I thought you guys would think I was crazy or try to talk me out of it. But for the last couple of weeks, I've been following Whale Boy's Facebook page and commenting as "Herman Whaleville." It's just really cool, Sara, all of the stuff that this one commenter "Salt" knows about whales and I know that it has to be James Turner on the keyboard. I feel like James is pretty much the only guy in our school who can have a conversation about something other than the Eagles, Instagram, Macklemore, or *Game of Thrones*. I mean, he's trying to save these really beautiful animals that everyone else is too busy to notice. And I like that he's got a passion other than CHS soccer. He's a little obsessive and weird, I get that. But aren't we all kind of weird in one way or another?

Anyway, I decided I would make this poster asking him to Turnabout and tape it to the desk where he collects funds for his Adopt-a-Whale project. So I did it today before lunch then I got in line with my donation right as James set up his cashbox. And I was hoping he'd see the poster and accept my invitation before there was a huge crowd. Some older hipster guy with too-tight jeans was standing videoing James with an iPhone, which was a little weird. And I turned around to talk to Becky. Then, Coxson and his crew passed by on their way to the cafeteria and burst out laughing. When I turned and looked at the poster, someone had added in pen, "Slap my tail, Whale Boy." The whole poster looked like some kind of practical joke. Coxson or one of his idiot wannabes totally defaced it. James looked at me and I opened my mouth. Even if I said something, Sara, he wouldn't have heard over the soccer team's laughter. It was horrible.

When it seemed things couldn't get any worse, they did. The hipster jumped out from behind his iPhone and headed straight for Coxson. The hipster might have hit Coxson or slapped him, I'm not sure which. In like two seconds, Dobson was on the scene and the hipster was being removed from the school and everyone was being herded out of the hall fire drill–style. So yeah, my asking was an epic fail.

Your Turnabout invite will fare better. I heard Sam tell Coxson in Bio that you asked him. Coxson cupped his hands on his chest (probably referring to your boobs) and gave Sam a fist bump. Sam said he was going to text you back tonight.

Love,
Sophia

From: dobsonjanman@yahoo.com
To: tbirdgoodlife@yahoo.com
Date: March 13, 2013 at 4:44 PM
Subject: CHS

T-bird—

There was major action today at CHS. An unauthorized
male entered the building for a second time this week. I
escorted him out only yesterday for videotaping students
without consent, and after the word-smacking I gave him I
can't believe the guy had the stones to come back again. But it
was him alright, wearing the same silver ring (jewelry on men
often an indicator of instability, as you know) and a different
badly-wrinkled shirt. Anyway, when the alert came through
on my walkie about an altercation in the hall, my first thought
was, "Fuck T-bird and his early retirement package. Jackass
is probably snoozing in his hammock right now." But the job
don't care what Kirk Dobson thinks. The job just is.

When I get on the scene, I see the intruder's about to take
out that little prick Charlie Coxson. Remember him? Drew
a two-foot dick on the faculty bathroom door in permanent
marker? I kind of wanted to let him get his teeth kicked in, but
not enough to risk my pension over it. Plus, Tedoni was waiting
for me to do something hero-like. I couldn't remember a thing
from that Taser training I told you about a few months back,
and I couldn't figure out how to get the damn safety off, so I
said screw it, and just went hands-on. Later Tedoni reminds
me that they don't like us to touch anyone anymore because
of lawsuits. I say if someone is going to sue me for doing my
job let 'em. I miss you, T-bird, 'cause we could laugh about this
shit. You got out of here just in time. This place is going to hell
in a handbasket. Did I tell you onion rings are gluten-free now?

Later old man,

Dobson

From: the.darren.olmstead@gmail.com
To: whaleboy4ever@gmail.com
Date: March 13, 2013 at 11:59 PM
Subject: RE: Hola

Jimmy Jam,

Just got back to Sash's house from police station. Neck
sore from Dobson's Vulcan death grip. Typing with left hand
only because icing right one which sore from where chopped
Charlie. Couldn't stand way he laughed at you. Cruelty in
eyes. No empathy or recognition that your feelings matter.
Plus, prank in general was messed up. One thing to be plain
mean to someone, another to use deepest longings to taunt
person. If someone made me think Corinne wanted me back
when really didn't, would freak. Plus, brought back memories
of bad times in high school with own version of Coxson. In
fact had more Coxsons than friends.

Anyway, was about punch him when realized was about
assault high school student, after lying way into school
pretending be legal guardian of made-up 15 y.o. cousin.

After getting kicked out previous day.

Am 23 years old.

Above series of realizations, plus fact actually hurting
him would only make him folk hero around school, plus fact
he's kind of big and no guarantee could beat him in fight,
interrupted muscle movements involved with punching.
Instinct to do something had already been engaged, though,
so punch morphed into strange karate chop–type movement.
Know nothing about karate. Landed first shot on top of head.
Shooting pain through hand indicated karate not learnable
by watching movies. Pretty sure hurt self worse than Coxson.
Pretty sure Coxson wiped cheek because was confused at
not feeling any pain, like guy in movie who thinks has been

shot but gun had blanks. Pretty sure getting dragged out by Dobson was best thing this point because have no idea what would have done next.

Explained everything to Mr. Tedoni while waiting for police. Nice guy for principal. Agreed not press charges long as never saw my face at school again. Still had go downtown because of prior arrest (will tell you later). Paid fine. Sash not happy to interrupt date come get me.

Feeling very sad as result all of above. About entire life. Ruined relationship with girl of dreams. Got fired from only job could get anywhere near industry want to work in. Screwing up pipe-dream documentary. Thought could help you. Sorry couldn't. Wasn't good at high school first time. Still not good.

Wish could be more like you. Have purpose, like your whales. At least got some good footage you handing out pamphlets before Coxson mess.

Hope some girl smart enough ask you Turnabout. See you Star Arcade tomorrow at eight.

D

From: craigdavidsmith2016@gmail.com
To: craigdavidsmith2016@gmail.com
Date: March 14, 2013 at 8:27 PM
Subject: One week ago

Dear Me,

Okay, that already sounds dumb. But what am I supposed to write, "Dear Craig"? As if I'm addressing a total stranger? I don't want to write "Dear Diary" either, because that makes it sound like there's somebody named Diary, which would also be stupid. Whatever, the point is, this whole thing is stupid and dumb. And so is Dr. Sizemore. Hey, that's kind of cool to write that since I know he'll never see it. Dr. Sizemore is a skinny balding idiot with creepy amounts of wrist hair that come past his long sleeves. He talks in this quiet, annoying way because he wants to seem "sensitive," when in fact all he's doing is trying to get me to trust him so that I'll tell him I got molested when I was six or something (in case anyone ever does read this, I wasn't!) and he can brag to his psychologist buddies about how he cured me.

Anyway, this little email diary was his dumb idea, but I promised my parents I'd try it, so here goes. I've got the alert thing set up to send this email to myself a week from today so I will have this record of how I was feeling a week ago. Which now will be in a week from now. It's like I'm in a really stupid time-travel movie or something.

Anyway, what stupid stuff have I been thinking about lately? Oh yeah, Turnabout is next week, and I'm going with Rebecca Vitello. She's cool. We're just friends, so it'll be pretty chill. I'm going to ride with Charlie and Liza and Doyle and Lissa.

Charlie's been kind of annoying me lately. First he was like, "Dude, you're good at Photoshop, you gotta put a blowhole and whale teeth on Turner's class picture." So I did that, then he's like, "Dude, you're good at research, find out some stuff about whale hunting so I can leave it on the Whale Boy Facebook page." So I did that. And he never even thanked me. Sometimes I think Charlie lives in a completely Charlie-centric universe and that we're all just floating in orbit around him. Whatever.

I just think it sucks that he doesn't appreciate me. Like I have nothing better to do than look up crap about whales and mess with pictures in Photoshop. Same with my parents. It's like they think it's easy for me to get a 2.9, play on the soccer team, and have a social life. And I have one little anxiety

attack, and now I've gotta go see a shrink and write letters to
myself, which makes it seem like they're trying to make me
even *more* crazy.

Okay, well, I was supposed to write this thing for at least
ten minutes, and I did, so now I'm going to be done with it so
I can start my essay on *Invisible Man*.

Signing off,

Me

From: ciaosoph@gmail.com
To: saraannblakely@gmail.com
Date: March 14, 2013 at 8:08 AM
Subject: Try Again

Hey Sara,

I'm in first period Italian, and we're supposed to be
listening to this audio book on the computer. But I can't stop
thinking about yesterday. I saw James Turner on the bus this
morning and I smiled. He pretended not to see me. I have to
do something about the whole Turnabout mess. Soon.

Anyway, last night, I was going to ask you what to do, but
your mom picked up your phone and said you were already
asleep. I don't talk to Anna Maria about boy stuff and Mom
was busy giving Baby a bath. So I went over to see Nonna. She
was asleep on her recliner in front of the TV (EWTN Global
Catholic Network) and some nun was still saying the novena.
I felt bad waking her up, but she didn't seem to mind. Nonna
made us caffè d'orzo, this decaffeinated drink that Anna
Maria calls imitation coffee, but it's really not coffee at all—
just steamed milk with roasted barley. I've loved it since I was
a little girl and no one makes it like Nonna. So we sat down
at her kitchen table. I was about to start talking about James

Turner and the Turnabout debacle when I happened to glance at a picture of me, Anna Maria, Mom, and Dad on the fridge from my seventh grade recital, and the next thing I know, I was talking about Albert and crying.

Nonna looked at me and pulled me to her. She whispered "*tesora mia*," "my treasure," and her breath smelled sweet like the anise seeds she likes to chew on sometimes. She hugged me, her housecoat warm from the caffè d'orzo steam. She's strong for such a little lady. Then we sat down and she told me how she spent a good portion of her own life living in the past, pretending that the war never came to Abruzzo and that she never had to leave the mountain town she grew up in to come to America. In her mind, everything in her town stayed the same as before she left. The oldest *signora* in the village still sat on the lip of the fountain in the piazza trading garlic for gossip. The little shrine to the Virgin still occupied the place where a little girl had a vision during a lightning storm. And the chair at her parents' table was still empty, waiting for her return. But then, Nonna went back to visit the town just a few weeks ago for the first time in years. The old signora was dead, an earthquake had destroyed the shrine, and her parents' house was occupied by summer vacationers from Germany. She looked at me and said, *"Hai capito?"* And you know my Italian's not great, but I got it. I understood everything Nonna said.

Love, Soph

From: saraannblakely@gmail.com
To: ciaosoph@gmail.com
Date: March 14, 2013 at 10:13 AM
Subject: RE: Try again

Soph-
   Got txt frm Sam after dr.'s appt. Time 2 book pedicures!

I know what ur g-ma's saying. I'll never dance the Sugar
Plum Fairy, never go 2 Juilliard. Prbly won't go 2 college
either. Hurts 2 bad when I type. Every skool paper lokz like
bad txt.

Luv,

Sara

From: whaleboy4ever@gmail.com
To: the.darren.olmstead@gmail.com
Date: March 14, 2013 at 10:36 PM
Subject: RE: Hola

Dear D-wow,

Did today really happen? Thank goodness the camera
was rolling or else I would be left believing it was only my
imagination. Did you get the look on my face? (Scratch that,
I forgot that I was wearing the yeti costume at the time.) Did
you get her on the bike as she turned off of King St. toward
Star Arcade? How about the cute way she kind of swung her
head from side to side as she pedaled like a little girl with a
song stuck in her head?

I have to tell you that I only realized the biker was Sophia
Lucca when she got close enough to Star Arcade that I could
see the glint of those gold rings she wears. I think I dropped
my 30 TOKENS FOR ONE DOLLAR sign. Sophia did
some talking. I can't remember much of what she said.

Something about Herman Whaleville. Something about
the poster at lunch. Something about handwriting. Something
about Coxson. Maybe you've got the transcript?

All I know is that she wants to go to Turnabout with me,
and she's going to wear a violet dress and she wants me to wear
a violet cummerbund, and instead of a corsage or boutonniere,
she's going to buy us matching Save-the-Whales bracelets.

I'm sorry that we didn't get to catch up after the shoot, especially because you seemed kind of down. My mom had pizza in the car and she didn't want it to get cold. But I wanted to tell you some good news in the hopes that it might improve your day. I saw this cool article about a whale named Valentina. This whale was caught in a prohibited shark net off the coast of Mexico in a National Wildlife Refuge. The situation was pretty grim. I mean, dire. And yet, with the help of some awesome, caring people, Valentina managed to get freed. And she lobtailed and breached in thanks. Things could've ended badly for Valentina like they did for Salt. But they didn't, not this time.

If I could lobtail for you, D-Dog, I would. Just saying.

Peace,

Jiminy Cricket

From: lwoodward1million@gmail.com
To: the.darren.olmstead@gmail.com
Date: March 14, 2013 at 11:25 PM
Subject: Letter

Yo D,

I was getting home from work yesterday, and I see this girl leaning over the windshield of your car and stuffing something under your windshield wipers. I thought you were getting a ticket or something, but this girl wasn't in a uniform.

Turns out it was the infamous Corinne. Wow, man. Now I can see why you've been so hung up on her. She's gorgeous. (A little on the granola side for my taste, but that's just splitting hairs. I mean, the tits . . .) She was leaving a letter for you, but I told her you were out of town and that I'd give it to you when you got back. See you in a couple days.

From: the.darren.olmstead@gmail.com
To: LWoodward@OneTermLife.com
Date: March 15, 2013 at 12:01 AM
Subject: RE: Letter

What?!?!?!?!

Dude, no! Overnight it! Wait, no. Forget it. I give you permission to open it. Just call me and read it out loud! Holy crap this is amazing! Fingers shaking. Can't believe I just admitted that. But I don't care! Wooo! Call me ASAP! In fact, call me ESTP (Even Sooner Than Possible)! Just make it happen!

Daaaaaaaaaaaaaaaarrrrrrrrrrrrrrrrrrrrrrrreeeeeeeeeeeeeeeeeee eeeeeeeeeeeeeennnnnnnnnnnnnnnnnnnnnnnnnnnnnnnnnn!

From: the.darren.olmstead@gmail.com
To: whaleboy4ever@gmail.com
Date: March 15, 2013 at 12:31 AM
Subject: All about Turnabout

Hey there Jamestin Turnerlake,

I reviewed some of today's footage, and as I understand it, Sophia was trying to tell you that it had in fact been her who'd been posting on Salt's FB page as Herman Whaleville, and that she had in fact penned the poster inviting you to Turnabout. Coxson only laughed when he saw it because he thought one of his buddies had made the entire thing, not just the "slap my tail" part. I had to listen a couple of times to put this together, because she was obviously really nervous about being on camera and was talking a mile a minute. I'll definitely have to include subtitles during that part. It's a great moment, though, for you and for the film. I'll interview you about it tomorrow, and then we can include voice-over of you talking about how you felt at that moment. A great second-act climax.

You were right in intuiting that I was down. Even the sight of you flippy-flopping around the ocean smacking your butt against the waves couldn't cheer me up now. My life is in that Dark Night of the Soul–type moment, where all has been lost, and the main character's hope is extinguished. This was brought about by the news that Corinne is moving in with her boyfriend. She wrote me a letter to let me know. She said she didn't want me to hear it from someone else, but I did anyway because I'm an idiot and had my roommate read it to me over the phone. Which was especially horrible because he tried to read it in a girl voice, like a movie or something where when someone reads a letter, the audience hears a voice-over of the character who wrote the letter. My roommate's really weird.

Anyway, let's now look at this rationally:

We haven't spoken in months.

I've been thinking about her less and less. (Really, I swear!)

She is happy. Good for her.

Now let's look at it entirely *irrationally*, which is how I'm actually looking at it:

EFF ME!!! Sure, I've been thinking about her less—less than ALL THE TIME! That's not because I miss her any less or want her back any less, it's out of sheer exhaustion, sheer self-preservation. My mind simply overloaded on thoughts about her. At a certain point, my body couldn't handle lying awake all night thinking about her, so I began to sleep again. My body couldn't handle not eating any longer, so it gave me an appetite. My brain couldn't handle the constant flood of images and thoughts about her, so it came up with some crazy distractions like flying across the country to film a documentary and try out experimental karate moves on teenage jerks. In other words, I never got over her; I just lost the ability to be as obsessed as I was.

Well, I just got it all back. Because you know what I realized? That despite all the evidence—the boyfriend, the trip to Spain, the expressing no desire at all to see me, the brief period where there was a *legally enforced buffer between us*, which I'll get to in a moment—I actually still believed, deep down, that we'd just hit a bump in the road. Not that I ever would have admitted that. I secretly figured that eventually she'd realize the error of her ways and come back to me. And to speed up the process, I planned on fixing the errors of *my* ways.

All of them.

Thus turning myself into an absolutely perfect human being. This perfection would cause her to, quite logically, want to get back together with me. Because who would turn down perfect? I got that crappy job at Testy Snobbin, I started lifting weights and stopped eating gluten, I started reading all the winners of the National Book Award in order. Out of some sense of charity I even started returning the emails of a weird kid who was obsessed with humpback whales.

CHARITY, James. Can you believe the effing arrogance of this? Exchanging emails with you, giving you advice, because I thought helping you out would make me a better person, make me more attractive to Corinne. You were going to be a bullet point on my imaginary perfect-boyfriend resume.

And I just want to promise you that that's no longer the case, and it hasn't been for a long time. Now I just think of you as my friend who's a lot younger. It's like one of those crappy romantic comedies, where the guy asks out the nerdy girl on a date as part of a bet (sorry, you're a nerdy girl in this analogy) and ends up falling in love with her. Wait, I'm not in love with you, I just want to make that clear. It was just for comparison's sake. I just think you're a cool dude. A very cool dude.

Anyway, the point is that—guess what?—I DIDN'T become perfect. I'm STILL not a god; I still have problems like everyone else, only probably way more. I'm still the same guy who Corinne got a 90-day restraining order against because I climbed in through her window to spread six dozen roses all through her house in an effort to try to get her back and then refused to leave when she arrived home with her grandfather, who she'd been out to dinner with. Old dude was snarling at me like a bulldog, and Corinne was near tears (the only time I ever saw her cry was when she was overcome with joy at a David Grisman concert—who can blame her? His version of "Shady Grove" is amazing), but I wasn't going to leave until I'd finished reading my list of seventy-two reasons we should be together (one for each rose). The cops showed up at #52 and dragged me out the door right as I was finishing #64. She said several times that she'd have to call the cops if I didn't leave, and I had HEARD her, but I hadn't actually LISTENED to her, which was why she'd broken up with me in the first place. Not listening seems to be a recurring theme in my life (see: my lone attempt at television writing).

I'm still the same guy who violated the order after 89 days because I just had to see if the new dude she was seeing was leaving her place on a weekend morning. I was sitting there in my car peering over a newspaper I was pretending to read, like I was on a stakeout in a cop movie, and she came out of her apartment—alone, fortunately, or things could have been much worse. She saw me before I could hide my face, and that's how I ended up in court again.

I'm still the same guy who got a killer lawyer (that my

dad paid for) who worked closely with a lenient judge who was
nice enough to sentence me to community service because
I quoted a Billy Collins poem he liked during my hearing
(my bestie from high school, Sash, who I'm staying with, is a
poet and got me into Collins). That's how I ended up in the
Resource Room at your school for a semester. Amazing that
they let a guy who was practically a stalker work with kids. But
my crime was truly a crime of passion, and at the time I really
thought I was acting in both of our best interests. I'm lucky
they were easy on me.

Anyway, at this point, I don't know what to do. I'm utterly
clueless. And I ask you, James, humbly, because you're my
friend and I honestly look up to you: How do I learn to feel
okay about all this?

D

From: whaleboy4ever@gmail.com
To: the.darren.olmstead@gmail.com
Date: March 15, 2013 at 12:57 AM
Subject: Symbiosis

Dear Da-Best:

It's past lights-out and I've already gone over my allotted
screen time for today, but I had to respond to your last email
posthaste. I have to admit—I didn't know what to make of
what you wrote in your correspondence at first, especially the
part about me being the nerdy girl.

Hence, I begin my analysis. At first blush, my gut reaction
to your email is that our relationship is symbiotic. In case it
has been a while since you've been in Bio, basically symbiosis
is a relationship between two species where one species
benefits at another's expense, where neither species benefits,

or where both benefit. At first, I wondered if our relationship was a type of symbiosis called commensalism where one species benefits and the other is essentially unharmed or receives a bit of protection from the first species. An example of commensalism would be whale lice (also known as cyamid amphipods). These little crabs hitch a ride to feast on the algae slime greasing a right whale's skin. The lice benefit from a free meal, and the whale is generally no worse for the wear—just a tad bit of damage to the skin (which helps researchers identify one right whale from another). My thought was that if our relationship was commensal, then I, of course, would be the right whale and you, well, you'd be the lice. But that didn't seem quite right to me.

Why?

Well, first off, we're not two separate species. Second, you're better-looking than these tiny crabs. Third, I'm not harmed by our relationship. Not even in the slightest bit.

In fact, the opposite.

Since we started emailing one another, I began healing from Salt's death, became arguably the most famous yeti in the tri-county area, waged a campaign to educate my fellow Carlsburg students about the plight of an endangered species, and got asked to Turnabout by the sweetest girl in the school.

Therefore, I've come to the realization that our relationship is one of mutualism, which is another type of symbiosis. A good example of mutualism is the boxer crab, which holds sea anemones (a kind of stinging coral that looks like a flower) in its claws to ward away predators. The crab receives protection because its enemies are afraid of getting stung, but in this case, the anemone benefits from the relationship too by getting first dibs at the crab's leftovers. This seems like our type of symbiosis because you helped me find my way in this aquarium called high school. Also, mutualism resembles friendship.

Which brings me to my next point. In order for our relationship to be considered mutualistic, I must do something for you other than be the nerdy girl or the Robin to your Batman. Thus, I want to provide some kind of advice to you now—how helpful it will be, I don't know. But it occurs to me that there is another interesting piece to symbiosis: mimicry.

Mimicry is where one animal mimics another for protection. The Indonesian mimic octopus, for example, can copy the color and shape of a lionfish, sea snake, or sole to avoid predators. This is a clever evolutionary adaptation because the octopus basically avoids certain harm from its predators that won't touch these other fish with a ten-foot pole. (I see your eyes getting heavy. Stay with me now.) In other words, the mimic octopus spends a lot of time being someone or something he really isn't.

Most people live their lives like the mimic octopus—because being more like others is just easier. Being yourself makes you vulnerable. And here's the thing that I most admire about you, Darren. You're not a mimic octopus. How do I know? Let's look at the evidence:

Exhibit A: You could have gone the easier road and coached ball like your dad or taken some boring desk job like your college friends, but instead you followed your interests and entered the film industry.

Exhibit B: You could have easily stayed at Testy Snobbin, unhappily fetching coffee and enduring boring sitcom plots until retirement. Instead, you decided to forge your own path, which meant making a documentary about a whale-obsessed guy.

Exhibit C: Even though making a documentary about me (of all people) to try to impress a girl seems a little crazy to me, I have to say, it is a pretty original idea!

I'm sure it makes no difference to you that this fifteen-year-old charity case thinks you're the kind of guy he'd like to be someday—blazing a life path without a second thought as to what anyone else thinks. And I can see how blazing said path could be lonely. Very. But that's why we animals need one another—whether we're the boxer crab or anemone, right whale or lice.

Sleep well, man. I'll see you tomorrow at the Arcade.

Your fan,

Jay

From: ciaosoph@gmail.com
To: saraannblakely@gmail.com
Date: March 15, 2013 at 7:25 PM
Subject: Albert

Hey Sara,

So I come home from school today and no one's in the house, but I hear voices in the backyard. Outside, there's Albert, wearing Dad's old work gloves, yanking yellowing weeds from the flower beds and throwing them into a pile. Mom snips at our hydrangea bushes with these ridiculously huge pruning shears. Nonna Rita stands with her hands on her hips, chaperoning. It's cold and almost dark.

I'm like: "What are you doing out here?"

"Cutting back," Mom goes as though she is suddenly an expert gardener.

Me: "Since when do we do that?"

Albert: "It's healthy to do every spring. Clear out some of the junk so we have a clean slate to work with."

Mom: "This summer, we might plant some roses." And her face is all shiny with sweat and happiness.

I shiver and go: "You're already thinking about summer?"

Mom: "Just dreaming about it, really. Albert's got a nursery catalog and we were looking through trying to plan things out."

Albert: "We were thinking some classic tea roses, like Pink Promise or Change of Heart, here. And your mom likes yellow. So maybe a bush of Monkey Business over there. We could even do some basil and tomatoes for your grandmother's famous cooking. What do you think, Sophia?"

After it becomes clear that I'm not going to respond to his question, Albert goes, "Getting cold out here. Why don't I take Rita inside?"

Nonna takes the arm Albert offers. She leans towards him as they walk toward the house.

"Nuh-ting gonna grow in dis soil," Nonna says. "Too many rocks."

Mom calls after them, saying she'll be in once she finishes with the last bush. I linger and that's when I notice the patch of earth where Papa and I once grew strawberries. The dirt is newly turned. Even though the wind is stinging my eyes, I wait a couple more seconds to see if Mom will remember. She continues to clip the bushes.

So anyway, what Nonna told me about the past and moving on and stuff . . . That's easier said than done.

Love,

Soph

From: the.darren.olmstead@gmail.com
To: whaleboy4ever@gmail.com
Date: March 15, 2013 at 9:16 PM
Subject: RE: Symbiosis

Hey there Semaj,

I know I told you in person already, but let me reiterate how moved I was by your last email. It really gave me the warm fuzzies all over. I would never have thought I could be so flattered at being told I'm not like an octopus. The way you framed all that stuff about how I've chosen to live my life made me feel like, "Yeah, I'm not just stumbling through life as if blindfolded and wearing one roller skate—I'm doing things my way! I'm like Frank Sinatra, baby!"

I'm pretty sure this idea wouldn't hold up under much scrutiny, so I'm not going to put it under much. With some stuff I think it's just best to think positively no matter what. So that's what I'm doing. Thinking positive. And I'm going to make this an awesome documentary, with full knowledge that it's not going to help get Corinne back. I'm going to do it because it's an end in itself, not just a way to accomplish some other goal. Just like I'm going to be your friend for no other reason than because I want your friendship, not as a self-improvement gimmick. Mutualism, dog. Love it.

Nerrad

From: sduckett@gnewc.org
To: pbrammer@gnewc.org
Date: March 16, 2013 at 9:00 AM
Subject: Tile?

Peter,

I was gonna try to fix that broken tile in your office. You in today?

—Stanley P. Duckett

From: pbrammer@gnewc.org
To: sduckett@gnewc.org
Date: March 16, 2013 at 9:40 AM
Subject: RE: Tile?

Dear Stanley,

Give that tile your best shot. The glue clearly isn't going to hold up and I am sick of tripping over it on humid days. I'm working from home.

Just had another false alarm yesterday with the investigation into my sister's disappearance. Apparently, human remains were found in a shallow grave in a remote coastal Mexican town whose name I can't remember, let alone pronounce. And for some reason, they thought it was Elsie. The detectives had me do a tongue swab and I was prepared to fly standby to Mexico to identify her body if need be. You'd think this news of Elsie's possible passing would make me sad, and it did. When I picture her in my mind, she's still nine years old and her blonde hair is pulled into two messy braids that she did all by herself. But I am also tired, Stanley. So if I'm being honest, I felt some relief at the officer's news as well, kind of like a caretaker might when a cancer patient dies.

Then the detectives called this morning, and it turns out that the bones do not belong to my sister. The DNA was not a match.

Best,

Peter

From: the.darren.olmstead@gmail.com
To: whaleboy4ever@gmail.com
Date: March 16, 2013 at 10:02 PM
Subject: Itinerary

All times approximate:

6 p.m.—Dinner at Sophia's grandmother's.

Did you give Sophia the release form to appear in the movie? I tell you, she's a great sport for doing it.

Have you been in touch with her grandmother lately? Have any idea how she might feel about being in the film? It seems that she's been a person who believed in you even when others didn't. From what you've said, I think she'll come off as a "wise but eccentric matriarch" type of character. And I can't wait to check out her pad. I'm hoping she's got lots of antique furniture and trinkets from the Old Country. There might be a parallel between her struggles as a young immigrant and your struggles as a whale advocate: both outside of the mainstream of your society, trying to stay true to your roots while participating in the weird customs of this new place, be it America or high school.

And I've been thinking about how awkward it could be, what with you being on sort of a first date, all dressed up, Sophia in a pretty dress and wearing makeup and too much perfume, and then of course . . . me. With a camera. So I figured that I'll go hang with Sophia's grandmother and help her in the kitchen while you guys are doing your awkward teenager thing, and I'll just leave the camera set up and rolling. It'll be weird at first, but you'll eventually get used to it, forget about it, and start being yourselves. Then after dinner, I'll do some over-the-shoulder shots of you guys talking but without the audio. Should work great.

8 p.m.—Dance.

As you know, I will be unable to attend, due to my tense relationship with Dobson and Principal What's-His-Name. But I'll be looking for a complete rundown of what happened after the fact. With Sophia, Sam, Charlie, all of 'em.

11 p.m.—Dance over.

BUT! As you don't know, I've got great news. An incredible stroke of luck. Remember how I told you my old buddy Sash is a poet? That's not the good news. The good news is that because he's a poet, he had to get another job because poets don't get paid jack, so he found work as a . . .

Wait for it . . .

Limo driver!

And he's driving me to the dance as soon as he picks up some tycoon from the airport and drops him at his hotel. I'll roll some film in back, and we'll get our ending, whatever that might be.

See you Friday,

Darr-Bear

P.S. Can I borrow a tie? I want to look respectable for Mrs. D'Angelo.

From: ciaosoph@gmail.com
To: saraannblakely@gmail.com
Date: March 17, 2013 at 1:18 AM
Subject: Tonight

Sara,

I missed you so much tonight! Sam said it was a last minute thing, that he showed up at your house and your mom said you weren't feeling well enough to go. Which sucks because that blue polish you got at our pedi appointment was going to match your dress so well. And your hair looked sooo awesome too. Just like Jennifer Lawrence's. I wish I could pull off that cut, but my cheeks are too "full" (which is *Glamour* magazine's way of saying "fat"). Anyway, it was kind of pathetic to watch Sam graze the snack table and make small talk with Mr. Tedoni during slow songs. So I'm not the only one who missed you.

Turnabout was pretty legendary. James actually had to take off his coat at one point because he was sweating, which was good. I was actually worried he'd not want to dance at all and it would be really awkward. But he had some basic crowd-pleaser moves and even danced to the Lumineers. You know the song that is not slow and not fast? Most of the cheerleaders sat it out, which tells you something. James was out on the dance floor though, rocking sunglasses thanks to the strobe lights triggering the Transitions lenses in his glasses. Anyway, I JUST got home (long story) and I'm exhausted and Mom is downstairs asleep in front of the TV which probably means I'll be grounded for life tomorrow. So if you don't hear from me, you know what happened.

Love,
Soph

From: whaleboy4ever@gmail.com
To: the.darren.olmstead@gmail.com
Date: March 17, 2013 at 1:30 AM
Subject: Dance

Hey D-Man,

It is after one o'clock a.m., and I'm trying to sleep, but I wanted to see if you were okay. I don't think you realized how numbed up your mouth was, so even though I'm pretty sure you told me the whole story, I couldn't understand a word you said. Plus, while you were talking, Sash had his phone on speaker as his boss was yelling at him about the limo.

In case you're worried, my parents didn't ground me for breaking curfew. I don't think that they ever thought such a thing would happen, so they didn't really have any punishment in mind when it did. Sophia might not be so lucky.

Anyway, given your dental emergency, we couldn't really talk about the dance. It's too bad that you were banned from school because you could have gotten rare (and I mean rare) footage of me cutting a Turnabout rug. Some of the soccer guys started chanting "Whale Boy." They made a little circle around me. Sophia started doing this little disco move and it inspired me somehow. I dropped to the floor, losing my glasses in the process. When I started to do the worm, this move I saw on YouTube, the crowd went wild. Epic, but I think I pulled a muscle in my back.

I hope you enjoyed dinner at Mrs. D'Angelo's house. You seemed a little flustered by her standing over you and repeating "*Mangia!*" Mrs. D'Angelo's harmless, but sometimes she feels more like a linebacker than a 4'11" grandmother. What about that gnocchi, though? Mrs. D'Angelo's an amazing cook. Did you shoot any scenes in the basement?

That is where the magic happens, man. It's something Mrs. D and I bond over—food.

I'm not sure how much you understood of your interview with Mrs. D'Angelo, especially once she got annoyed with finding words in English and switched to Italian. I'll give you my best translation (which is probably not much better than what you'd find online given that I am a B– student). Basically, Mrs. D'Angelo was born in a tiny town in Abruzzo, Italy. (Read: larger population of sheep than people.) Her father was a goldsmith and the village mayor so Mrs. Lucca's family enjoyed local celebrity status. Then World War II broke out and she was sent to America with a man from her village who had started a life in South Philly. She never really wanted to leave her village, but her new husband was her only connection to Italy. They didn't have much, she said, but they had each other.

Signing off,
Whale Boy

From: saraannblakely@gmail.com
To: ciaosoph@gmail.com
Date: March 17, 2013 at 8:01 AM
Subject: RE: Tonight

Soph,

Dance=epic! Sad I missed.

When getting ready, couldn't remember last time I talked 2 Sam in person @ skool. Or anyone other than u. Then pain started. Felt bad b/c mom was supposed 2 drive us.

Luv ya,
Sara

From: the.darren.olmstead@gmail.com
To: whaleboy4ever@gmail.com
Date: March 17, 2013 at 8:49 AM
Subject: RE: Dance

Hey JameSession,

I'm a little dopey right now from painkillers, so forgive me if I ramble a bit. Here's what you didn't see that led to all this nonsense.

Sash and I had left the limo in front of the gym to step out and grab some nachos and a Slurpee over at the 7-Eleven down the block from your school. We're on our way back, slurping our Slurpees, noshing on our nachos, and Sash all of a sudden gets super-inspired because he's loving the nachos so much, and he's like, "These things are unbelievable. I need to write a poem about them." And I'm like, "Sash, I'm pretty sure no one writes poems about nachos." And he's like, "William Carlos Williams." And I'm like, "I have no idea who that is." And he's like, "Nobody ever wrote poems about red wheelbarrows either, but then he did and it was awesome! Nachos are going to be my red wheelbarrow." And I've been friends with Sash since freshman year of high school and thus am used to this sort of thing, so I'm like, "Totally." And he launches into this stream-of-consciousness free-form verse about 7-Eleven nachos, talking about the cheese, thicker than blood and smoother than ivory, and the plastic tray, made of fossil fuels forged in the Earth's crust for thousands of years for the express purpose of being refined into this sturdy clear container and holding this glorious combination of corn chips and processed cheese foods.

And it was strangely compelling there for a minute, until we're nearing the car and he says (again, I'm paraphrasing), "And that you, glorious nachos, should be available to us so readily and for a price so reasonable is a gift for which we should all be grateful. As some marvel at a sunset, I marvel at—WHAT THE HOLY HELL! OH GOD NO!"

The all-caps section is when he notices the long, looping line of missing paint from the side of his limo. It was clear that someone had keyed it badly. Like, really badly. Immediately I knew it was Coxson or one of his cronies. When we rolled up to drop you guys off earlier, I was watching (and filming) from inside the limo and I caught his reaction. Dude looked like Kermit the Frog, he was so green with envy! Poor Mr. Soccer Stud, watching you step out of a sleek limo with the lovely Sophia on your arm. Then he noticed me and threw a major sneer my way. (Which I can't totally blame him for—I did karate-chop his head three days ago.)

That sneer was all the evidence I needed when I saw that scratch on Sash's limo. So when kids came pouring out of the dance, I had to step up to him. Sixteen years old or not, that kid had to be dealt with.

We were already up in each other's faces, I think, by the time you came striding out with Sophia. (Even in my teen-icidal rage I did notice that you guys were holding hands; nice work.) And man, what a clever little jerk that Coxson is. I was like, "You're gonna *pay* for this, you little shit." And he was like, "Go ahead, hit me." And I was like, "No, I mean, you're going to pay for this, as in all your lawn-mowing money now belongs to Watson Limo and Transport Service. Give me your mom's email address." It didn't occur to me how un-badass a response this was until it came out of my mouth, but it was too late then. Coxson stepped even closer, so we were literally toe-to-toe. I could feel the tips of our shoes pressing together. And he looked up at me and said, "Bro, you snitchin'?" Like he was a gang member or something and I had just turned him over to the police. I busted out laughing then, realizing that, oh yeah, I'm dealing with a freaking *kid* here. The little jerk has no idea what he's doing.

Right in the middle of my little bout of laughter, that's when he sucker punched me.

He can throw a punch, I'll grant him that, especially for a guy who specializes in a sport where you mostly use your feet. Soon as I fell over I could feel that tooth floating around in my mouth. Otherwise I would've—well, I don't know what I would have done. Slugging a sixteen-year-old, given that I'm still on probation for the whole incident with the roses, wouldn't have been the best move.

Messed up as that was, I'm just thankful I was able to turn the camera on once we got in the limo and narrate our trip to the emergency dentist. I think it's gonna be riveting footage.

I'm just about packed up and ready to head to the airport. It's been real, James. Whatever that means.

Keep it authentic,

DarrenPain

From: whaleboy4ever@gmail.com
To: the.darren.olmstead@gmail.com
Date: March 18, 2013 at 9:05 AM
Subject: RE: Dance

Darren,

It is weird but I had a feeling something bad was going to happen to you. I don't know if you noticed, but before the dance when we were having dinner at Mrs. D'Angelo's, she brought out that bowl of water and the bottle of olive oil. You know how Mrs. D'Angelo dropped olive oil into the water and then said that blessing with her hand on your head? Well, it was because she said you have the evil eye. From what Sophia tells me, the evil eye is like a curse. Bad crap starts happening to you. No need to worry though, Mrs. D'Angelo took care of you and reversed the curse. Life should start looking up. Hopefully, that will be sooner rather than later.

Later,

J-ded

From: the.darren.olmstead@gmail.com
To: whaleboy4ever@gmail.com
Date: March 18, 2013 at 10:45 AM
Subject: The Movie

Hey Earth James,

It's Sky Darren. I'm writing you from our cruising altitude of 30,000 feet. I have no business paying for Wi-Fi on a plane, but I couldn't help myself. I get too bored and antsy on planes if I just sit there. So now I'm emailing you and listening to the Stones on Spotify. Mick Jagger keeps telling me that he can't get any satisfaction and that you can't always get what you want. To which I say, "You're preaching to the choir director, bro!"

So Mrs. D thinks I have the evil eye! Just my luck, right? I think it was our conversation in the basement that led her to that conclusion. I got to talking, somehow veered into the Corinne thing—imagine that!—and Mrs. D'Angelo just kept rolling her hand over in the air and saying, "Go on," so I guess she understood. So I told her the whole saga of my last couple years: the breakup, the restraining order, the community service, you, Testy Snobbin, the end of Testy Snobbin, Corinne in Spain, Corinne cohabitating with this new shmuck. And when I finished, damn near out of breath because it was the first time I put into words all the shit that's been knocking around inside my brains for the past couple years, she waved her hand and started leading me over to the corner where there was this old bureau. When we got there, she picked up this framed black-and-white picture of some guy wearing suit pants and a white T-shirt and holding a baby. It was one of those pictures from way, way back, from before people smiled for pictures. The baby looks bored, and the dude just looks tired. He's wearing suspenders over a T-shirt. I've always loved the T-shirt–and–suspenders look. It just screams "grumpy old man" even if the guy's not old.

"My husband," she said. "When I have him, I strong. I happy." She turned the frame facedown on the table, looked back up at me, and said, "When he die, I am no as happy . . . but I am now stronger." She made a muscle with her arm, pointed for a second at it, then up at her heart. She stared at me like she was waiting for something, and I thought I got what she was talking about, so I nodded real gravely, as if she'd just dropped major knowledge on me and I was instantly changed forever.

That was a bunch of cow dung, though. I had no idea what she was talking about or what it had to do with me. But now that I've had a chance to think about it, I think I do.

Look at my life: I'm a dude in America of sound body and with a college degree. No one close to me has ever died. My great-grandparents were dead before I was born, my grandpa on my mom's side died when I was seven and I barely remember him because they moved to Arizona to avoid winter, and my other three grandparents are all still kickin'. My point is, losing Corinne was about the first time I've really lost anyone. I've never had to deal with something like Sophia has. And she had to do it as a teenager. Can't imagine how hard that'd be.

I've had other breakups, but this is the first real-deal one. So, loss sucks. But maybe I can come out of it a little sadder but a little tougher. Doesn't sound like the worst thing, especially if when the next loss comes—and more will come, no avoiding them forever—I'll be a little better prepared as a result. And maybe the next good thing in life will seem a little more precious knowing that it could be gone at any moment.

God, that all sounds maudlin. Straight up last-scene-of-an-episode-of-*7th-Heaven* (don't tell anyone; if you've seen it you know what I mean). But I think Mrs. D'Angelo is evidence I'm right. Look at how much she likes you and Sophia. Went on about you guys' little date as much as I went on about Corinne. Personally, I would've been more comfortable during a rectal exam than I was watching you two eating garlic bread and making the most god-awful awkward small talk I've ever witnessed. (Actual snippet I remember. You: "I really like this bread." Her: "Bread is good." You: "Yeah, it really is. Unless you have a wheat allergy." You know you're approaching Peak Awkward when the conversation has turned to wheat allergies.) Not you guys' fault. Product of your age. I was the same way. Actually no. I was equally awkward, but I just kept talking and talking as if hoping that my words could somehow outrun my awkwardness. (They couldn't.)

Much as it pained me to listen to you guys, Mrs. D'Angelo thought it was the most adorable damn thing in the world and would have stayed up there longer if she didn't have to check on the pignoli.

Point is, she can get a kick out of stuff like that, I think, because she's lost enough in her time to appreciate how badly you guys are grasping for something, trying to make some sort of connection. I guess it only made me want to vomit because here I am almost ten years older than you, and I'm pretty much in the same boat.

Well, metaphorically speaking. Physically, I'm on a plane, which is now preparing for its descent, so all the seatbacks and tray-tables must be put in their upright positions and I've got to shut down this computer machine.

Later,

Descending Darren

From: whaleboy4ever@gmail.com
To: the.darren.olmstead@gmail.com
Date: March 18, 2013 at 4:12 PM
Subject: RE: The Movie

Dear Darren:

Did we kiss? Read on.

While we were at the emergency dentist, wondering what had happened to you, Sash was on the phone with his boss, cursing up a storm. It was weird how everyone in the waiting room was looking at me and Sophia in our formal clothes, so we went back to the limo and talked for a while. Actually, Sophia talked. I slipped off my dress shoes. And as I poured Sprite into a champagne flute, Sophia was going: "Oh my God, I'm going to be in so much trouble for breaking curfew. My mom's going to kill me. Or worse, she'll talk to Nonna to come up with some completely insane punishment like taking my phone away for the weekend. Or making me go to 6:30 a.m. Mass every morning for Lent. It's going to be bad, James. I mean, she told me like fifty times before I left to be home by midnight. That she'd be waiting up." There was a two-second silence where I wondered if I should comment. But Sophia was like a whale surfacing for air. After she sucked in a breath, she was ready to dive right back in. "But it's like who's Mom to judge me anyway? She's the one who stayed out till one in the morning with Albert Stevens last week. I'm not deaf. I could totally hear the key in the front door and their laughing. Honestly, James, I don't know what she sees in him, you know? The teeth, the roses, everything. He's nothing like my dad."

Sophia picked at her nail polish. In the quiet, I hummed to a David Archuleta song that was playing on the radio. (Don't tell anyone I watch *American Idol* and I won't say a word about *7th Heaven*). With the changing colors of fiber optic light, I noticed Sophia's eye makeup had smeared into an abstract watercolor painting—you know, the kind that is hard to understand but also wildly beautiful. And I knew I should say something to her, but we never rehearsed any role plays in Social Skills that would actually be useful like how to talk to a crying girl who is cool enough to wear a Save the Whales bracelet. As you probably know by now, I'm no good without a script.

So I just hooked an arm around Sophia's bare shoulders. She cried a little more and I could feel her melting into me. Her forehead was so close that my lips grazed her skin. And then her face tipped up toward mine and we were kissing. Or rather she was kissing me. I didn't know what to do with my mouth or my hands or my tongue. But Sophia didn't seem to care. For five glorious seconds, I swallowed her breath and she swallowed mine. It reminded me of this awesome (and kind of far-fetched) account I once read from 1918 where a guy, a real guy—James Bartley—spent hours in a sperm whale's belly. Bartley went completely nuts after the crew of his whaling boat extricated him alive and now I can understand why. He'd been somewhere he never thought he'd go—deep inside another creature. Somewhere he might never go again.

In the middle of this magical moment, you yanked open the passenger-side door of the limo and dropped into the seat. Sash followed, yelling into his phone about "fucking vandalistic miscreants." You kept groaning as you held your ice pack up to your mouth. It kind of killed the mood.

There's something else I wanted to tell you in case it is helpful with the edits for the documentary. As we were leaving Turnabout, Sam slung his arm around my shoulder and slipped an envelope into my blazer pocket. I didn't open the envelope up until just now when I emptied my pockets to take the coat to the dry cleaner. You'll remember how I told you that Coxson, Sam, and the rest of the soccer team stole my diorama for Bio at the beginning of this year and defaced it as part of some bizarre hazing ritual. Well, as you might recall, I included my one and only picture of Salt in the diorama and I figured it ended up in the cafeteria dumpster with the rest of my project. Just now though, when I opened the envelope that Sam gave me at the dance, the lost picture of Salt was inside. The photo was crumpled and there was a smudge of ketchup on the fluke. But still.

Your friend,

James

P.S. I finished putting in my time to pay for the new Abominable Snowman costume at Star Arcade yesterday. They let me keep the old yeti gear, the one stained with jungle juice from Smith's party. Just for shits and giggles (Urban Dictionary, 2013), I tried the old Abominable Snowman costume on the other day, and this is crazy, but it barely fit. I must've had a growth spurt.

From: ciaosoph@gmail.com
To: saraannblakely@gmail.com
Date: March 20, 2013 at 8:30 PM
Subject: Starbucks

Dear Sara,

So I'm only allowed out of the house for school-related stuff. Becky and I went to the Starbucks on King St. today because we had to finish our Bio homework. We're sipping on our Fraps and laughing and rehashing the latest episode of *The Bachelor* when I look two seats in front of us. And . . . there's Albert. His back is to us, but I would recognize his bad hair and misaligned ears anywhere. Anyway, I tell Becky, and instead of talking about theories of evolution, we're making fun of Albert for the next hour and a half. How he's such a loser to sit by himself, how he keeps wiping his face with a handkerchief (what—is he from 1910?), how he is drinking chocolate milk at a coffee shop, on and on. I start feeling kind of bad when we move on to ragging on his ride, this hulking handicap van parked right out front, because I know the reason why he drives that beast: his mom.

Anyway, when Becky's mom comes to pick her up, we've accomplished nothing, so I decide to stay and actually do some work then take the Pace home (don't tell anyone!). Thanks to the Frap, I need to pee, but since peeing means walking past Albert's table, I hold it. I try to study, but there's this worm of guilt that keeps digging deeper and deeper under my skin. When I can't hold it any more, I walk by Albert's table on the way to the bathroom, hoping he won't notice me. He doesn't. Because he is looking at a brochure about hospice and wiping tears from his eyes. And I know it has to be for his mom. The only other time I saw a grown man cry was when my dad was diagnosed with cancer. Mom had to hold him up under the arms, Dad cried so hard about it being stage IV. Anyway, on the way back from the bathroom, I can hardly walk. I feel like I am made of glass or something breakable. I pause at Albert's table and say hello. He looks up and sniffs. I point to the brochure and say, "Sorry," even though I hated when people said that to me. And he hugs me, Sara, and I don't know why but I hug him back, and he's still sitting and I'm standing, and his head is on my chest, and I'm crying and he's crying, and he's holding on and I'm holding on. And finally the barista offers me a tissue and tap water. I know that I'd already made a complete fool out of myself so I don't even think twice about accepting when Albert offers to drive me home in that horrendous van. I'll call you about next weekend.

Love,

Soph

From: saraannblakely@gmail.com
To: ciaosoph@gmail.com
Date: March 20, 2013 at 9:21 PM
Subject: RE: Starbucks

Hey Soph-

Was ur barista @ Starbucks named Wes? Cute and kinda short? He's used 2 tears. That's where Mom and Dad took me when we got the test results 4 JA. At least he didn't offer u a free drink.

L8r,

Sara

From: craigdavidsmith2016@gmail.com
To: craigdavidsmith2016@gmail.com
Date: March 21, 2013 at 9:00 PM
Subject: RE: One week ago

Dear me,

Me again. Well, it's interesting to see what you, I mean I, wrote last week. I was pretty pissed about having to write this email journal. And it was pretty funny rereading that line about Dr. Sizemore's creepy wrist hair. The session wasn't as bad this week, except for his whole "sensitive voice" thing. I called him out on how fake it was because it was annoying me pretty badly. He said, "I think I know what you mean, but I don't know if 'fake' is the right word. But I will readily admit that I'm adapting to my role as a counselor. In that role, I would like to be a calming presence for my patients, but if you were next to me on the sideline as I cheered on my son at his soccer game, you'd hear a much different voice." Then he kind of turned it around on me and said, "Do you ever find yourself modifying your behavior based on your social situation, or do you speak and act the same way with your friends as you do with your parents and teachers?"

"Of course not," I said. "Kids who do that are the ones who have to take social skills classes to learn how to have a conversation."

"So it's not necessarily a bad thing to adapt your behavior to your role in a given interaction?"

"No, not necessarily."

"What roles do you think you and your friend Charlie play when you're together?"

Only now do I see what he was doing there, how he slipped Charlie into the conversation because I'd mentioned him a couple times in last week's session. I'll hand it to

Sizemore this time. You got me to talk. You win.

I didn't tell him that I'd been thinking about pretty much that exact question ever since Turnabout. But I told him how it went down. The ride situation got all messed up because Sara's mom was supposed to drive them but Sara bailed and Sam ended up riding with Becky and me. And right away, there was this sort of relief that I wasn't with Charlie. Which is weird. We've been best friends since fifth grade, so it was strange that I was glad he wasn't with us. But without him around, there wasn't this worry every time I spoke that he might try to one-up me. I swear, I could tell a story about getting kidnapped by aliens, and he'd be like, "That's nothing compared to this one time when I got kidnapped by aliens . . ."

When we got to the dance, as Sam was climbing out of the car, this envelope fell out of his jacket pocket. I grabbed it off the seat and it said James on it. I asked Sam what it was, and he gave me this sly smile and said, "Tell you later." After that I basically forgot about it. But during the dance, this little dance circle broke out, and there's James Turner right in the middle of it, going nuts. I mean, it wasn't like good good, but his enthusiasm was like a fourteen out of ten, like he was a baby or something and had just discovered that there was this thing you could do with your body called dancing. It was one of those things where you're sort of embarrassed for someone and a little happy too, because that kid usually acts like such a stiff. People were going nuts cheering him on. And right in the middle of it all, Charlie comes up to me and tells me about the limo (I haven't mentioned the limo to Sizemore, because if he told my dad I might never play soccer again). I was like, "Why? What did Turner do?"

And Charlie was like, "He only came here with the old video camera creeper who tried to kill me the other day—no big deal."

"Don't you think maybe you're exaggerating a little?" I said.

"He karate-chopped my head! Just because he sucks at karate doesn't mean he wasn't trying to kill me. We can't let him get away with it."

I didn't really want to do it, but I remembered the envelope that Sam had, and I figured it was part of the plan too, a little continuation of the stuff I did to Sophia's poster. And Sam's super nice usually, so I figured if Sam was going after Turner he must really deserve it. I was going to go ask him, but Charlie was telling me I had to go out to the limo right then and do it before more cars showed up outside the gym.

Oof, that scraping sound. Way worse than fingernails on a chalkboard.

Now I don't know what's going on, because ever since the dance Sam won't talk to me, and I don't really feel like talking to Charlie.

Hope you're feeling better by this time next week,
Me

APRIL 2013

From: whaleboy4ever@gmail.com
To: the.darren.olmstead@gmail.com
Date: April 5, 2013 at 2:12 PM
Subject: RE: The Movie

Darren????
    Everything okay?

From: whaleboy4ever@gmail.com
To: pbrammer@gnewc.org
Date: April 5, 2013 9:09 PM
Subject: Follow Up

Dear Mr. Peter Brammer, PhD:

    Thank you for the email you sent a month or so ago and my apologies that I am just now responding. I have been busy both scholastically and extracurricularly.

    First, I wanted to let you know that I did not raise the funds I sent to GNEWC myself and I feel it unfair to take even a lion's share of the credit. In fact, my fellow students at Carlsburg High were instrumental in contributing to the cause that we both care so much about, and they really deserve the appreciation for the $5,346.27.

Second, I am pleased to hear that the donation has been put to good use and that your research may yield some answers in what caused those six whales to beach last year. As you may remember from our brief phone conversation at the time of crisis and my many subsequent inquiries thereafter, I was very concerned about one juvenile in particular named Salt. Has your team determined a cause of death yet? I am guessing either parasitic disease or sonar interference played a role, but I am only an amateur cetologist, not an expert like you.

Sincerely,

James Turner

P.S. Did you receive the other funds I sent?

From: pbrammer@gnewc.org
To: whaleboy4ever@gmail.com
Date: April 13, 2013 at 4:12 PM
RE: Follow Up

Dear Mr. Turner:

Forgive my delayed response. I've been out in the field for the past few days and I completely forgot to turn on my out-of-office message. Yes, we did get the other donations, and I am sorry that once again no one acknowledged these gifts sooner. This afternoon, I put a thank you note addressed to your fellow high school students in the mail. Your humility with regards to your role in the fundraising effort is, I must say, refreshing and it helps revise somewhat my unfavorable opinion of your generation as self-absorbed and entitled.

Regarding our research, we are making some good headway. I expect to meet with the team in the next few weeks to go over our initial conclusions—at which time I will get back to you. I appreciate your interest, as our work can be quite isolating and we can forget that we are not alone in our efforts to protect this vulnerable and intriguing species.

Best,

Peter

From: the.darren.olmstead@gmail.com
To: whaleboy4ever@gmail.com
Date: April 26, 2013 at 9:48 PM
Subject: Hey

Dearest J-Man,

Sorry I've been out of touch. Congrats on the growth spurt.

I believe I may have had a sort of emotional growth spurt since my visit to Philly. At least I hope so. With me, it's always hard to tell. While knowing full well that the best way to move forward is to put one foot in front of the other, I tend to take a step forward, then one backward to where I started, then a couple at odd diagonals, then I do an ungraceful pirouette, and generally stumble through life as if I'm drunk or, if you're a teetotaler, have a really bad inner ear infection.

In this case, as always, it was adversity that pushed me toward a deeper understanding of myself. Which really gets my goat. Why can't I become a better human being during a period of relative calm, in which I eat oatmeal with fresh berries every morning and go to the symphony occasionally? Not that I've ever had such a period. And it actually sounds a little boring, now that I think about it.

Anyway, it started on my plane ride home. Freaking airlines. Forced me to check my carry-on bag at the gate because I was in Zone Seven Thousand and they ran out of room in the overhead bins. Then, as I imagine it, the baggage handlers proceeded to use my bag as a tackling dummy in an impromptu football practice in preparation for their big game against the ticket counter people. At least that's what it looked like when I got my bag back.

And of course, what was in there?

My hard drive.

With all the footage I'd shot of you on it.

Completely shot. Took it to a data recovery place and everything. No dice.

As I'd committed a considerable amount of money, a fair amount of time, and an INSANE AMOUNT OF DREAMING to the documentary, I was understandably vexed by this occurrence. In this instance, "vexed" is the diplomatic way of saying that I subjected a whole host of airline employees to a tongue-lashing that would make drill sergeants blush.

And then I had a meltdown.

Kind of like the one I'd had when Corinne broke up with me, but this time it was actually a little bit worse. Because, of course, I still had hopes that making this amazing documentary would impress the hell out of her and make her want me back, even though I'd sensed that tendency earlier and tried not to fall into the trap. And aside from that, the doc meant a lot to me because you and your story mean a lot to me, and I wanted to share it with other people so they could see what a cool little dude you are. I've grown a lot through our correspondence and friendship—there, I said it, I'm friends with a fifteen year-old (cue an old lady clutching her pearls, "Oh my!").

Anyway, I was miserable for a few weeks, sitting around watching movies every night, eating like crap, buying weird crap I saw on infomercials (if you ever need a water clock or a boot and glove dryer, let me know), and generally hating my life.

And the worst part was that I had some real problems that didn't directly involve Corinne, and of course the only person I wanted to confide in about them was Corinne. But I knew there was no way I could start spending time with her and whining about all my problems to her, even if she let me. I'd just end up getting hooked on her again.

So I made a movie.

Written by Darren Olmstead. Produced by Darren Olmstead. Directed by Darren Olmstead.

Starring Corinne.

It was the hardest project I've ever been involved with, even though I conceived it and shot it in about five minutes. I handed her the script, asked her if it looked right, and she said it did. I asked if she'd be in it, and she looked up at me with this sad smile that contained more than a hint of pity too. I didn't care. I knew what I needed to do.

Here's the entire script. She said it just as I wrote it. No changed lines, no improvising.

"Darren, you're a good person, and we had some great times together, but I'm happy in my new relationship. However, you need to know that even if this relationship ends, you and I aren't going to be together. We had our time, and that time has passed."

I'd like to thank the Academy . . .

I have a private link to it, and if I ever feel myself starting to pine for her, I pull it up, watch it (sometimes a few times), and get my head straight. It can actually be a calming experience. Maybe I can become the guru of Rejection

Meditation. Anyway, for now it's my own *Seven Up*. I just hope I don't have to keep making them every seven years.

Anyway, that's where I'm at. It's not the perfect place, but I don't think there is one.

I hope you're doing well and that you're still loving and advocating for whales. And I hope you're being good to Sophia and she's being good to you. That's all you can really try for, right? Say hi to Mrs. D'Angelo for me.

Your friend,

Darren

Let me say that again:

YOUR FRIEND,

Darren

From: whaleboy4ever@gmail.com
To: the.darren.olmstead@gmail.com
Date: April 27, 2013 at 5:02 PM
Subject: RE: Hey

Hi D—

I'm sorry to hear about the hard drive, especially after all that you went through to make the doc. It sounds like your resulting project, though painful, was maybe even more meaningful. But I must admit that I was getting strangely excited to see how I would look on the big screen. Sophia gave me some pictures from the dance and the purple cummerbund was kind of sick (Urban Dictionary, 2013).

Speaking of Sophia, we've been hanging out pretty often. We made a pact that if I went to her dance recital in June, she'd take a tutorial on cetaceans with Prof. Turner (aka me!). So far, she's addicted to old Cousteau videos, but *Whale Wars* gives her a tension headache. I figure one out of two isn't bad. We're also doing our Honors English project together, which means that I actually had to read *Moby-Dick* and relive the cruelty of turn-of-the-century whaling. (Quick history lesson: in New England alone, hundreds of thousands of sperm whales were massacred to make candles so that we humans did not have to endure darkness. Three-quarters of the sperm whale population was gone by the twentieth century when Americans started plundering the earth instead of the sea for energy.) The report is actually about the book's author, Herman Melville, who I wanted to hate pretty much from the get-go. But it turns out Melville spent a lot of time on ships in his youth where his fellow crewmen made fun of him for his middle-class clothes and manners. I guess you could say he was kind of an outcast. Sophia and I even found this quote about his experience at sea: "I found myself a sort of Ishmael . . . without a single friend or companion." Not exactly the villain I made him out to be in my mind.

We're about halfway through the report, mostly because Sophia still talks A LOT. But sometimes there are these lulls in the conversation where we bob in silence like two separate buoys and I don't know where she is or what she is thinking. I used to like those quiet moments when we were deep inside ourselves, but now they scare me a little. Because I wonder: can you really ever know a fellow creature, even of your own species, the way you know yourself?

Your friend,

J

From: whaleboy4ever@gmail.com
To: pbrammer@gnewc.org
Date: April 27, 2013 at 6:41 PM
Subject: Advice

Dear Peter Brammer, PhD:

Thank you for your email. I received the thank you
note and shared it with the Carlsburg High donors via social
media. They particularly enjoyed the picture you included of
"our" pod of whales breaching—385 Likes on Facebook. As
you know, I am interested in devoting my life to saving these
interesting and beautiful creatures. Based on your own career
path, I am wondering if you could offer any advice to me.

Sincerely,

James Turner

From: pbrammer@gnewc.org
To: whaleboy4ever@gmail.com
Date: April 28, 2013 at 10:12 AM
Subject: RE: Advice

Dear Mr. Turner:

Call me Peter.

I am glad that the students enjoyed the photo. I took it
myself when the pod emerged from the waves. The initial
report on the 2012 beaching of several juveniles is almost
complete and I will send a photocopy to you in the mail once
it is available.

As for career advice, honestly I don't know what I could
tell you that you couldn't find on the Internet these days. That
said, I am reminded of a story that I feel compelled to share.
I grew up in Alaska near an Inuit community, and part of the

native people's mythology included a tale about Big Raven, a deity in animal form. Humor me while I recount a bastardized version of that story. Here we go:

One day, Big Raven was flying along the coast when he encountered a whale stranded on the shore. The whale was flailing and struggling for life, which the Inuit see as a sign that the universe is in disorder. But what could one little bird do to save such a behemoth? In his quest to help reverse the whale's fate, Big Raven tugged at the whale's fluke, but the creature wouldn't budge. So the bird asked for the Great Spirit's help and he was told that if he ate certain mushrooms in the forest, he would gain enormous strength. So he scurried to the shady woods and gorged himself on fungi until he felt he would surely be too heavy to fly. Racing back to the beach, he pulled the whale once more toward the sea. This time, the whale slid across the sand, slipping into the cold waves. And so it goes, one tiny raven rescued a giant.

This myth inspired me to get through Organic Chem in college and my orals in grad school. It even came to mind at different points of struggle in my personal life. But now, at 37 years of age, I no longer believe in Big Raven the way I once did. And so, the advice I now dispense to you, young man, is this: no one person alone can save anyone or anything.

Best,

Peter

From: whaleboy4ever@gmail.com
To: pbrammer@gnewc.org
Date: April 28, 2013 at 3:52 PM
Subject: RE: Advice

Dear Peter:

Thank you for the advice. That myth is pretty incredible, but I will try my best not to hero-worship Big Raven.

If you have a moment, I actually wanted to ask you about something whale-related that I've been thinking about for a long time. Last fall, when I was bored in the library during study hall at school, I plugged "whales" into a search engine for fun. And this old 2004 *New York Times* article grabbed my attention. Apparently, a 52-hertz whale has been roaming the North Pacific since 1992, emitting a low *basso profundo* sound, which the article said is equivalent to a tuba's lowest note. Researchers know that the noise is coming from a whale, but it is not the voice of any KNOWN whale. Odder still, the creature is travelling alone—not in a pod—and its frequent vocalizations go completely unanswered. One researcher said, "The call, possibly a mating signal, suggests that the animal lives in total, and undesired, isolation." The scientists have suggested that this whale may be malformed or perhaps a cross between a blue whale and some other species. What do you think? The group that put out this report is right up the road from you at the Woods Hole Oceanographic Institution. Has your team formed an opinion on their findings? Could the 52-hertz whale really be the only one of its kind in the whole world?

I await your response.

Sincerely,

James Turner

ACKNOWLEDGMENTS

A big thank you from Natalie to:

Rich, for reading bad first drafts and supporting my writing habit by cheering me through grad school, encouraging me to attend residencies and conferences, picking up the slack around the house when I was holed up on the computer, and pushing me to continue when I was ready to give up. Ten years to forever.

Patrick and Henry, remember James Turner and always be you.

Mom, for taking me on my first whale watch and teaching me pretty much everything I know. For traveling across the country to help me realize a dream. Love to you and Sal.

Dad, who will always live in my memories, and for our time by the sea.

Leslie, for being my reader.

J T-H, M T-H, J T-W, and S T-W, for listening.

Grandpatty and Grandad, for the countless hours of diaper changes, games of pony boy, and park hopping with H. Thanks for helping me to continue my career.

My University of Chicago Writers' Studio colleagues and teachers, for the workshops that honed my craft.

Jim Heynen, who helped me find my voice.

Adrianne Harun, for the keen insight and editorial advice on "Whale Boy."

Suzanne Berne, who I look up to both as a mentor and person.

Debby Vetter, for publishing "Whale Boy," and the Society of Children's Book Writers and Illustrators for the honor.

Sara Crowe and Andrew Karre, for their enthusiasm, guidance, and wisdom. You guys rock!

Stan Rubin, Judith Kitchen, and the entire RWW community (including Kristina and Liz), for residencies that inspired.

Bill, who wrote me an email awhile back that said: "Tell me if you have any interest in this: We start a serial correspondence as characters." LOL.

—Natalie

A big thank you from Bill to:

Mom and Dad, for everything, nothing less.

Mike, Sharon, Kathy, and David, for helping give me a childhood that bordered on idyllic, and plenty of advice since.

Manolo Celi and Peter Fontaine, for watering the seed.

Jenny Sanchez, for being my first collaborator.

Scott Nadelson and David Huddle, for their wonderful mentorship.

Matt Holloway, for being "in this thing" too.

Andrew Karre, for getting it.

Jay, for liking to read.

KL, for so much and so many kinds of support.

Stan Rubin, Judith Kitchen, and the entire RWW community, for fostering such a nurturing and challenging environment.

Natalie, for rolling with this strange idea, and for writing the first entry in our exchange.

—Bill

ADDITIONAL INFORMATION

Some great sources of information on the topic of whales consulted during the writing of this novel included: "*Song of the Sea*, a Capella and Unanswered" by Andrew C. Revkin of the *New York Times*, *The Secret World of Whales* by Charles Siebert, *The Birth of a Humpback Whale* by Robert Matero, and *The Whale: In Search of the Giants* of the Sea by Phillip Hoare.

ABOUT THE AUTHORS

Natalie Haney Tilghman first published the short story "Whale Boy," which inspired the character of James Turner, in *Cicada* magazine. In 2010, she won first place for fiction in the *Atlantic Monthly*'s Student Writing Contest. She has an MFA in creative writing from the Rainier Writing Workshop. She lives in Glenview, Illinois, with her husband, two sons, and their Chihuahua. Visit her at www.natalietilghman.com.

Bill Sommer writes fiction and screenplays and plays the drums. His work has appeared in the *Whitefish Review* and in the New Libri Press *Coffee Shorts* series. He is the screenwriter of the film *Tony Tango*, winner of Best Feature Film at the Chicago Comedy Film Festival. He has an MFA in creative writing from the Rainier Writing Workshop and a Bachelor's degree in jazz performance from the University of Miami. He is the drummer for the band Book of Colors and for singer/songwriter Ed Hale. Born and raised in Saint Louis, he now lives in Atlanta. This is his first novel.